THE
GIRL ON
THE
MOON

S0-BDT-498

a novel of endless time

JULIE MANNIX
VON ZERNECK

with
KATHY HATFIELD

Printed in the United States of America
Blue Blazer Productions, Inc.
c/o HJTH
450 N. Roxbury Dr. 8th Floor
Beverly Hills, CA 90210

ISBN 978-0-9857358-5-2

Dedicated to my family

To Frank,
who hears me and sees me like
no one else in the world can.

To Kathy,
who found me when I was lost
and whose love and stories
helped to inspire and shape this book.

To Danielle,
whose gumption and spirit
guide me and make me brave.

To Francis,
who singlehandedly has taught me
that all things are possible.

"To see a world in a grain of sand
and heaven in a wildflower.
Hold infinity in the palm of your hand,
and eternity in an hour."

William Blake

PRELUDE

POPPY sped her rented car down the winding driveway, not noticing the overgrown pasture on one side and the now-failing orchard on the other. As she slammed on the brakes, stopping within a foot of the old stone house, the dirt scattered and danced beneath her tires. It had been many years since she had been in her childhood home.

The house looked the worse for wear. The roof seemed to sag and the thick green paint on the front door was chipping and curling away. When she smashed the knocker against the front door, it came off in her hand.

"I know you are in there. I know you two are there. I can see your cars," she screamed out angrily. Throwing the heavy knocker to the ground, she began beating her fists against the door. But still there was no answer.

"I'm coming in," she yelled as loud as she could, as she went around toward the shed door, knowing it would be unlocked.

She was so furious that her heart felt like it was flying around inside her. "You think you can hide from me," she bellowed. "But I'm going to get some answers from you now," she called, as she raced around to the back of the house. Flinging open the rickety shed door, she pushed her way in.

Moving quickly from room to room, she passed by two old and tattered slipcovered chairs that sat by the fireplace. There was a huge television now, she noticed, where a very small one had once been. But her father's priceless leather-bound books still held their place of honor along the walls, though the floor-to-ceiling shelves holding them were now at an awkward tilt. "How dare you try and hide from me," she screamed.

"Where are you two?" she shouted, as she bolted back out into the hallway and then ran up the stairs two at a time. "I called you. I warned you. I left a message. You knew I'd be here." She was like an irate bull that after decades and decades had finally been let loose from its pen.

Slamming open the first door at the head of the stairs, it crashed with a bang against the wall behind it. Stepping inside, her eyes darted around. It had been her room once, but she could tell her aunt Jane had taken it over by the stacks of newspapers that covered every surface. The bed had been left unmade, the sheets thrown back.

"I'll find you," she yelled out, her voice cracking with rage, as she tore out of that room and raced down the hall into the one across the way.

It was in her parents' room—her mother's room now—that she found them at last. The door was open and she went right in. There they were, side-by-side, fast asleep on the bed.

She took in the sight of them. Even in old age they were still beautiful, both dressed in matching rose-colored silk nightgowns, their white, glossy hair like radiant halos around their heads.

"Wake up," she screamed. "Wake up. I'm here."

They did not stir. Poppy yelled and screamed then,

unleashing all her rage and sadness, saying everything she had waited so many years to be able to say.

When she finished, exhausted, she suddenly felt weak. Her knees started to give out from under her, and she reached for the doorjamb to steady herself. It was then that she heard the bewildering, beautiful sound. It was like a hum. A hum that first encircled her, and then clung to her tightly, like a wet sheet draped around her body.

And she understood. Her mother and her aunt were not sleeping. They were dead. A great sorrow overtook her.

Suddenly she noticed, for the first time, all the red diaries scattered around her mother's bed.

Just when Poppy thought it was finally over, she realized that this was not the end, but the very beginning.

There is always one moment in childhood
when the door opens and lets the future in.
- Graham Greene

CHAPTER ONE

THE YEAR was 1439. Lucienne Badeaux genuflected in front of the main altar of the small church in Paris. Turning right, she found the modest altar to St. Anthony, hidden away in the shadows. St. Anthony was her saint— the saint she prayed to whenever in need. Kneeling down, she slid off her gloves to bless herself. She noticed the stains of cobalt blue and flaxen yellow on her fingers and palms. She had neglected to wash her hands in her haste to get to the church before night fell.

"I am sorry I am late," she said, looking up at the sweet face of her favorite saint. Tears rolled down her eyes. Tears not of weakness, but of pleasure and power and pride. "I have finally finished it," she whispered. "My very own painting. Thank you for helping me and giving me the courage to do it."

It was bitter cold outside. The streets had been almost empty when she'd run through them, wrapped tightly in her heavy crimson cloak. It was the harshest winter she could remember. Hardly anybody ventured out unless forced by circumstance. But she had promised her mother that she would light a candle for her father, who had died on this day the year prior. Gustave Badeaux had died a happy man. He had died a famous man—one of the most famous painters in Paris, in fact. But he had not died a wealthy man, because he was hopeless at managing his funds. Although she had loved her father and had mourned his passing, she and her mother had been obligated to keep his death a secret. Everyone thought he was working somewhere in the countryside. Little did they know that she had inherited her father's gift and had taken over for him more than a year before his death. In that time, he'd taught her carefully, knowing that his work would go on after him, and his family would be provided for.

Only Pascal knew the truth. There was no way to keep it from him. Not only did he take care of the horses and tend to the land, he helped mix her paints. Together, they went to the fields in the spring and summer to pick the flowers that they ground into pigment. "You should make your own art, as well," Pascal had whispered one day. "Sign it with your own name and not your father's."

My own art, she had thought late at night, and her heart had skipped a beat. As much as the thought had excited her, it had also made her fearful. *What if I am not capable of anything other than being just my father's substitute?*

She heard a noise behind her. The groundskeeper was beginning to close the large, wooden church doors for the night. She would have to hurry. She lit the candle closest to the statue of St. Anthony. Rising, she ran to the doors and slipped out, just before they were shut and locked.

The moon was in the shape of a crescent that night. Against the dark black of the sky it looked as if it was close enough to touch and bright enough to blind. Her father would have liked this moon, she knew. She bowed her head in reverence to its beauty.

When she looked up, all she saw were their eyes glowing in the dark. She could hear their low, throaty growling, see their bared, white, knife-like teeth. Years later, books would be written about the pack of wolves that took over Paris for three months that year.

Taking a step backward, she turned and beat hard on the church doors with her fists. She called out for help into the cold and empty night, but no one came. She fell to the ground, holding her cloak up to shield herself. She could smell their sharp odor as they approached—softly, elegantly, deliberately. The pain she felt lasted only a second.

She died almost immediately. She was their first kill.

∞

When she lifted her arms, she noticed the lack of resistance. She could feel with her mind and think with her heart. She was no longer cold or afraid. She spread herself wide-open and saw that the edges of her melted into the expanse.

"Where am I?" she asked the shadows gathered around her.

"You're home. You're back," they told her. "Nothing is forever. Not even here. Not even this. We come, we go, and we are back again. We are ever-changing. Like the beam of light that bounces off the top of a white tin roof to become the fluff on the end of a dandelion, to be blown away by the breath of a child."

She felt suddenly that all things were right and good. She began to hum.

∞

Pascal waited at the front door. Lucienne should have been back by now. She knew how dangerous it was to be out after the sun had set. He wished he had not listened and gone with her, but she was headstrong and had insisted. She wanted to be alone. Sometimes, when she'd leave, he would follow her to make sure she was safe. But today, just as he was about to go after her, he had been called away by Madame Badeaux. Now, having finished his work, he decided to meet her halfway.

As he hurried along the cobblestones toward the church with the single steeple, he heard something and stopped. *What is that?* he thought to himself. *It sounds like someone humming. Where is it coming from?* he wondered. He stood listening as the snow fell lightly around him. Soon, the humming came to a stop, but the memory of it would stay with him forever.

Later, Pascal stood under the window, by the wooden desk that had once belonged to Lucienne. The palms of his hands moved along the uneven wood. His heart no longer felt like it was beating. He could no longer catch the scent of the paints that lay around, unused now for weeks. He felt no cold, despite the snow piling up outside; he heard no sounds; he saw nothing. Nothing at all. There was nothing for him anymore, now that she was gone.

∞

She looked in, a snowflake clinging to the window, and

saw the lonely figure of Pascal grieving for her. She yearned to go to him, to take his anguish away.

"We are none of us ever alone," the shadows whispered, holding her back. "We are all linked, attached, part of everyone and everything. We are all fragments in a limitless design."

∞

Pascal picked up Lucienne's brushes and washed each one carefully. He arranged her palette, her tools, her mortar and pestle. He did not notice that the sun was coming up, and when its unexpected brilliance shone through the window, it startled him. He stepped back. It was then that he saw it, the small canvas lying half-hidden at the far end of the table. He went to it and picked it up. A smile crossed his tear-stained face. It was an exquisite painting of a cobblestone street surrounding a small church with just a single steeple; the sky, a cobalt blue, and the fields beyond, cast in flaxen yellow. He recognized it immediately. It was the church on the steps of which she'd taken her last breath. On the bottom right corner it was signed, simply, *Lucienne Badeaux*.

Pascal took Lucienne's painting and put it in his small room. There, he could glance at it as soon as the sun came up every morning, and again when he blew out his candle each night.

∞

Her heart swelled beyond its capacity. The moon, the sun, and the stars all paused. The earth stood still. She felt herself liquefy into a stream. She flowed into a river and disappeared into the sea. A drop amid a hundred

8

thousand waves, she traveled on a golden breeze.

Then, on the feather of an eagle dipping for fish, she journeyed through deserts where lizards roamed. And she found herself on a shivering mountaintop, where shaggy winter-coated goats wandered. Transforming into the beat of a drum, she became the spark of a heart in love. In this way, ages passed.

And then, in chorus, three brilliant flames appeared. They were magnificent bursts of turquoise, sapphire, indigo blue. "Who are you?" she inquired. "We are parts of you," they chanted, their voices harmoniously suggesting something familiar. Then she remembered. Then she knew.

The flames pulled her through centuries, into occasions yet to be. They reeled, they swayed and they soared. Always together, always rejoicing as one.

When she first felt the pull, heard the murmur, the whisper, the irresistible plea, they were lingering on the edge of a precipice.

"What is happening?" they inquired, alarmed. "You are fading. You are wilting," they cried. "You are starting to disappear."

"I am being called," she told them. "I have no choice. When we are summoned we must go. Do not be fearful. We will be together again soon," she assured them. Then, reaching out for the closest heavenly body, she pulled it to her and upon each of the three, she left the mark of the moon.

If you are not too long,
I will wait here for you all my life.
- Oscar Wilde

CHAPTER TWO

THE COVERED porch was dripping with morning glories. Sitting in a wicker chair, Jewell was reading a book of poetry. Soft blossoms fell onto the brim of her wide straw hat, the shoulders of her white lace dress, and then into the cup of tea she was sipping. This made her laugh.

When the first pain hit, she put her book aside. "It's coming, I think," she said, a glow of exhilaration overwhelming her face.

Collier, in the wicker chair next to hers, looked up from his papers. His pen froze, and he smiled. This would be their first child. They were ready. Everything was prepared. He rose, helped her up and led her inside, stopping once to kiss her cheek.

The doctor was there by the time her deep moaning began. It was a speedy birth, with no complications. Jewell's sister, Jane, appeared just as the baby was born. Entering the room unnoticed, she gently and firmly removed the slippery infant from the doctor's arms, and bundled her up in a soft, pink blanket. Holding the baby close to her heart, she took in a breath of her newly-born fragrance. She smelled like cherry blossoms, and vanilla, and a magnificent field of poppies. Then, as though the child were her own, she smiled down on her with enormous pride. It was only after the doctor cleared his throat that she finally surrendered the infant into her sister's outstretched arms.

○○○

The year was 1946. The baby was born remembering. By the time she was able to talk, she had forgotten it all.

Baptized at the Church of the Holy Apostles by Father Sean Patrick, a family friend, Josephine Penrose Russell was the answer to her parents' and aunt's prayers. Growing up on Philadelphia's Main Line, Poppy, as everyone called her, was loved dearly by them all. Her father was a writer of historical fiction who traveled all over the world for research. He was often accompanied by her mother who, along with her Aunt Jane, was a writer of books about baking. Sometimes six months passed between visits from her parents, so, really, it was Aunt Jane and Uncle Fitz who brought her up.

She was very fond of them. Uncle Fitz was an eccentric man whose family owned coal mines and steel mills in Pennsylvania. He loved fox hunting, and would ride Poppy on his shoulders to meet the hounds every Saturday morning. While Poppy felt loved and safe in the care of her aunt and uncle, she longed for her parents nevertheless. Sometimes, she would go to bed imagining that she was with her parents, wherever they were, and cry herself to sleep.

Without the pressure of parental demands, however, she had a freedom most children did not have. Aunt Jane did not require that Poppy take French or Latin lessons, ballroom dancing classes, or piano, as she herself had been forced to do in her youth, and had detested. Whenever she wanted, Poppy could run naked out into the rain and cavort in pools of squelchy mud. She raced her little white Shetland pony, Chiclet, as fast as she could and was encouraged to paint with her watercolors on a long sheet of paper that wrapped around the wall of her playroom and extended out to the hallway. She drew castles and flowers and children climbing trees, but mostly she painted the night sky, and masses of twinkling stars. Her Aunt Jane found a pattern for a painter's smock and had it sewn for Poppy out of black fabric. She gave it to her for her sixth birthday with a wicker basket of bright new paints. "It's the best present I ever got," Poppy screamed with joy when she opened the box. No one stopped her when, that very night, she woke up and wandered outside in her black painter's smock, carrying her basket, and waited for the moon to send down a staircase so she could climb up and paint what was up there, too.

By the time Poppy was a tall and lanky eight-year-old, she had developed an imagination that took her to places that most children she knew weren't able to find. She was a day-dreamer and a night-dreamer and a dreamer of fantastical things.

o o o

Everything that her mother had, her Aunt Jane had, also. They had the same blond hair, the same blue eyes, the same dimple in the chin, the same long body, long fingers, the same precise way of speaking. They even had the same sweet smell. Really, her aunt and her mother seemed to be one and the same. They were one person, in two different bodies—one body made of brilliant flames and fire, the other full of sweet spice and everything nice. So much did Poppy belong to both her mother and her aunt that it never concerned her when she found herself hugging one and it turned out that she was embracing the other.

Besides their physical similarities, the other thing the sisters had in common was their love of sweets. When Jewell wasn't away on her travels, she and Jane would spend hours in each other's kitchens covered in dustings of white flour, fingers dripping with chocolate, smelling of cinnamon and burnt sugar and cloves. They wrote and published the first of many cookbooks, *The Kindliness of Sweets*, when Poppy was just a toddler. They wrote in the very early mornings, after their daily walk. Early morning was their most treasured time. They felt ageless then, surrounded by the tools of their trade: paper and pen, mixing bowls, rolling pins, and beautiful, white marble pastry boards. It was together in the kitchen, in the early mornings, that their senses were most pure. They felt totally connected then. Like nothing could come between them.

ooo

Poppy could vaguely remember when she first began to mimic her mother and aunt, walking behind them whenever she could, mirroring them, reflecting their every move. But she could only do so much. No matter how well she succeeded at imitating them, she could never actually *be* them. There was an invisible force that linked her aunt to her mother. It was a force she would never be able to rival.

One Christmas morning, Poppy was given two

identical Raggedy Ann dolls. She named the one her aunt gave her Raggedy Honey. The other, from her mother, she named Raggedy Sweet. She tied them together at the waists with a piece of red twine and turned them into Siamese twins. She had tea parties with them, took them on carriage rides, and chatted to them all day long. At night though, when the lights were turned off, she untied them, hanging the red twine on her bedpost until the following day. Sometimes Raggedy Honey slept on Poppy's heart. Sometimes Raggedy Honey slept under the bed, and Raggedy Sweet slept on her heart. In that way, Poppy could be alone with just one or just the other.

ooo

After her parents settled back down for good on their farm in the house with the covered front porch from which the morning glories hung, they decided it was time for Poppy's first Holy Communion. Father Sean Patrick, the family friend who had baptized her eight years before, prepared her for the special day by teaching her catechisms and certain prayers. On the day the sacrament was to be bestowed on her and twenty others, her mother and aunt dressed her in a splendid white taffeta dress, a white tulle veil, white stockings, and white satin shoes. "I'm a bride. I'm a bride. I'm getting married today," she sang, as she twirled in front of the mirror until she was so dizzy she had to lie down. "Do you remember your First Communion?" she asked them both. "Yes," they answered together. In her dizziness they looked like two twinkling angels, and she thought that maybe this might be the happiest day of her life.

When the sacred moment finally came for Father Sean

Patrick to put the host on Poppy's slippery tongue, she was terrified that because she was trembling so hard, it would slip off and land on the floor. She'd heard that it had happened to a boy, and that a week later he had been run over by a cement truck, and his soul had gone straight to Hell. Whichever child had told her this story had gone on to say that the boy's soul hadn't even stopped in Limbo, and that the same fate awaited his parents.

Poppy was horrified that the same would happen to her. So, the moment the small round wafer was set on her tongue, she snapped it in like a bullfrog and closed her mouth, firm and tight. With a sigh of relief, the host still safe on her tongue, she followed the girl in front of her back to the pew. But just as she was about to kneel down, she saw stars, an entire circle of them.

"My host," she said when she woke up. "You fainted," her mother whispered.

"But where is it? It's not in my mouth. It must have fallen out!"

Immediately, Aunt Jane began to search around on the floor. Spotting the white round host, she picked it up.

"Open your mouth, Poppy," she whispered, and she quickly slipped the holy host in.

On the car ride home, Poppy whimpered the whole way, constantly asking if she was now going to go to Hell.

"No. You are not," her mother, who was driving, said sternly. "Though your aunt might make a quick visit there."

Her aunt leaned over and murmured very softly into Poppy's ear. "There is no Hell, Poppy," she said. "But there is a Paradise. And that is where we'll all be going someday."

15

Time flies over us, but leaves
its shadow behind.
- Nathaniel Hawthorne

CHAPTER THREE

THE OLD stone house that Poppy and her parents lived in was beautiful, surrounded by acres and acres of green, rolling land. But the ancient boilers in the basement seldom did their job of heating the big place, and much to Poppy's delight, now that her parents were always home, the fireplace was in use from the middle of autumn to the beginning of spring. It was in the living room filled with four generations of books that she would stretch out on the Oriental carpet, and listen as her father read to her for hours on end, while her mother edited the pages he had written that day. She loved glancing up at her father from time to time, sitting in his green leather chair by the fireplace. His voice was so strong, so solid, that it made her feel secure. She liked studying his hands. They were strong, too, but long and lean like the rest of him. He had a tattoo on his upper right arm. No other father she knew had one. It was of a flame. He told her, when she asked, that it was like the flame inside of him that made him want to write. One thing she knew about him, now that he was home for more than a month at a time, was that he didn't like fuss. That was what her mother called it. Fuss.

"It's my job to organize and control things so fuss doesn't happen. He needs quiet and calm," her mother revealed one day while the two of them made peach and apple cinnamon pies together. "A lot of silence. That is why we have come home to live. Traveling is hard on him," she explained. They had gathered baskets of both fruits in the orchard nearby and were now taking step-by-step photographs with a camera on a tripod, for a new book her mother and her aunt were writing. "I liked the traveling, though. I loved it, in fact. All those marvelous people, all interesting, all so full of adventure. It was stimulating." Poppy snapped pictures as her mother expertly sliced the apples and then the peaches and mixed them together. "But it was just too much for him after a while," her mother went on. "So here we are. Home again, home again, jiggity jig, with me making pies!"

From what Poppy could tell, not many other mothers were like hers, and of that she was very proud. She loved everything about her mother. She loved the way her mother talked. She loved the way her mother drove fast, hitting each bump on the winding country roads, causing Poppy to bounce. She loved the way her mother rode her bay mare like she was a jockey coming in for the finish at the Kentucky Derby.

"She likes speed," Aunt Jane would tell her. "She always has. I, on the other hand, don't. Your father's the same way. It's opposites that attract. It would be like having light without dark. Heat without cold. We all need a counter weight to hold us to the earth."

ooo

The year Poppy was nine, her father was writing a book based on the little-known true story of a pack of starving wolves who took over Paris for three months in the winter of 1439. A year later, when her father's publisher delivered the finished book, he gave Poppy a copy. Curled up in the over-stuffed chair in her bedroom, she turned to the first page. At the top, above the first chapter heading, was a picture of what looked like a little square in Paris, with a winding cobblestone street surrounding a small church with a single steeple. She stared at it for quite a while, somehow remembering it, though she was certain she'd never seen it before. She asked her father if she could have a copy of the picture for herself. "I'll try," he said.

Right from the start, her father's book captivated her. At the same time, however, she found it extremely upsetting. On several occasions, she was forced to put it down because it gave her horrific nightmares in which she could sometimes even smell the scent of the wolves.

Months later, she received something in the mail with foreign stamps on it. It was addressed only to her. When she opened the box and pulled off the paper around it, she found a small painting inside. She was dumbfounded. It was the picture she loved so much from her father's book. The sky in the painting was a vibrant cobalt blue and the fields beyond the church, lit by the sun, were a golden, flaxen yellow.

"It's the original painting," her father told her, taking the picture from her, and holding it up to the light so he could see it better. "It's absolutely beautiful, isn't it, darling?" He placed a kiss on the top of her head and then went on proudly. "The artist was a woman, which was very uncommon in those days. Her name, as you can see on the bottom right side, is Lucienne Badeaux. Her father was the painter Gustave Badeaux."

Poppy hung the painting on the wall next to her bed, where she could look at it upon rising every morning, and then again just before falling off to sleep at night. She studied it carefully for hours sometimes, holding a magnifying glass close to it so she could scrutinize each tiny detail.

When her father came to visit her in her room one night, he found her examining it once again. "It is, and always will be, the most important thing ever to be mine," she confided in him with tears in her eyes.

∘∘∘

By the time Poppy graduated high school, she knew Spanish and Latin reasonably well. Spanish and Latin were easy for her, but French, for some reason, was more difficult. Her mother could speak it fluently and her father could speak it enough to join in, so twice a week they spoke only French at breakfast and dinner. "S'il vous plaît, passer la sauce et aussi la chaussure," Poppy requested one evening. "Je suis ce soir tellement faim que je pourrais manger..." Before she could finish the sentence, the gravy bowl was placed on the table in front of her, which was followed by her father's polished, size 11 cordovan shoe. She looked at her mother and then burst out giggling. "All right, all right, let me get my dictionary. Thank God I'm not in a fancy restaurant in Paris somewhere."

Poppy was good at tennis, and could play the piano well enough to please herself. This was all because of her mother, who, upon her return years before, had convinced Poppy to catch up on all of these things. But what really gave Poppy pleasure in her high school years was writing. She would stay up late at night outlining stories, dream about them, and then wake up early in the morning and write them down without hesitation, as the sun came up. And she knew, without a shadow of doubt, that this was her path. This was the course she had been set on. She had found her passion, and just like her father, would devote herself to her art no matter what obstacles stood in her way. She wrote stories for the school newspaper and also a few that she sent to her father's agent. "You are good, Poppy," he wrote back. "Keep going and keep sending." She received the literary prize at her commencement at the end of her senior year. "I am so proud of you," Aunt Jane said, reaching to hug her. "I know that's the only prize you really care about." Poppy held the scroll in her hands and nodded, squeezing her eyes tightly together to keep back her tears.

After being presented to society at a lovely debutante ball, she went off to Vassar College. It was there that a scout from *Seventeen* magazine saw her running across campus, overloaded with books, her long, athletic legs carrying her through the crowds, her blond hair trailing like a veil behind, her skin, smooth and radiant, her intense blue eyes fixed on the path ahead. The scout would later describe her to the editor as a presence who stood out among the hundreds around her, as if a light were focused just on her. And, what's more, she was completely oblivious to her own beauty. If asked, Poppy would say of herself, "I wish I were more interesting-looking rather than so run-of-the-mill pretty. I do have a scar on my chin from a riding accident, though, which is my only saving grace." After the magazine that featured her photo and an interview about her studies and ambitions came out on the stands, Poppy was encouraged to sign with a modeling agency. "I would far prefer to write for the magazine than to have my picture in it," she confessed. What she did not share with anyone except Aunt Jane, however, was the fury she felt at the headline above her picture on the cover: *Aspiring Author Eager to Follow in Her Father's Famous Footsteps.* "I am not my father's shadow," she told her aunt. "I was born to write."

Her life was going the way it was intended to go. The way her mother had carefully planned it. However, careful planning rarely guards against the whims of fate, she was soon to find.

A jug fills drop by drop.

- Buddha

CHAPTER FOUR

"HELLO," he said, reaching out hurriedly to shake her hand. His brown eyes were filled with excitement as they turned to hers for a minute and then looked away, searching the office for someone or something else. His thick, dark hair was disheveled from having run his hands through it a dozen times. His shirt was already wrinkled, his tie was askew, and his sleeves were rolled up like he had put in a full day, though it was still early morning. He was very unlike the privileged boys Poppy had known on the Main Line. In fact, he had more energy in his little finger, she decided, then all of them put together.

"I'm Aristotle Doumas," he introduced himself. His back was to her now, and he was walking fast. As she followed closely behind, she couldn't help but notice his physique was lean and compact as he moved. Her pulse began to race. "We are delighted to have you aboard for the summer," he called to her over his shoulder. "As you can see, we are very busy right now. We can certainly use your help." Then, stopping abruptly, he turned back to her and without warning he handed her the thick file of papers he had been carrying all along. "Oh, yeah, make ten copies of these for me, will you please," he hesitated a second. "Judy? Jennifer?" Immediately she came to the rescue. "Josephine," she said. "Actually, no, it's Poppy, really. Poppy Penrose Russell."

"Well, Poppy Penrose Russell." He laughed. "The copy machine is over there against the wall. But get me a coffee first, will you? Black with four sugars. I'm Greek, I like things sweet."

Poppy couldn't help staring after him as he walked away. Aristotle Doumas was the most stunning man she had ever seen. His Bronx accent was strong but had a tinge of a European flavor mixed in, which made it unusual. His hair was dark and had a way of falling over one eye. He had high, chiseled cheekbones, wide-set dark brown eyes, and full lips.

Her heart was beating hard as she went to make copies of the thick file of papers he had handed her. Black with four sugars, she thought. Her hands were shaking so hard she wondered how she would ever manage to carry a cup of hot coffee to him without spilling it on the way.

○○○

Aristotle Doumas's parents and brothers were killed in 1946, in an explosion during the civil war in Greece. Orphaned, he had managed to find a group of older refugees, with whom he made the harrowing journey to America. He was just twelve years old. The family who took him in owned a coffee shop in the Bronx. When he wasn't in school Ari had worked there in the early mornings and late afternoons. A few years later, the family had expanded to several more coffee shops, and Ari worked in all of them, as well. Not only was Ari a hardworking boy but he was smart as a whip, too. He had come over from Greece speaking English, Greek, French and Italian, had graduated high school a year early and received a full scholarship to Colombia University. Though a junior editor at a very prestigious publishing house now, he was on his way to becoming a well-known book publisher, he assured everyone around. There was something about this man and his lust for life that drew her to him. That she was interning at a publishing house in New York was enough excitement for her already, but by the end of her first day there she had also fallen in love.

A week later, while strolling through Central Park on a lunch break, Poppy noticed Ari seated on a bench near the fountain in Columbus Circle, reading a manuscript. She couldn't stop herself. She walked over and sat down right next to him. Without a word, she took out her lunch and boldly offered him half of her sandwich. "Thank you, Poppy Penrose Russell," he said. And with a grin that left her feeling faint, he took it and ate it in several bites. After that, they met at the same bench almost every day. They talked and talked. Aristotle Doumas fascinated her. They talked about their childhoods, their families, their hopes, and their dreams. He wanted to know everything about her. Every detail of her life was interesting to him. She had always been uncomfortable talking about herself. But with Ari, it was different. She wanted to be known by him. Being together felt like the most natural thing in the world. It felt right. It felt true. It felt destined-to-be.

It wasn't until the end of the summer, when it was time for Poppy to return to school for her sophomore year, that she discovered she was pregnant with Ari's child.

When she told him, she saw a black mist come into his eyes. His face turned pale. "I have a confession to make," he told her. And her heart stood still.

○○○

After she heard the words, *I'm married*, she stopped listening. Everything around her began to blur. She couldn't see. She couldn't hear. She couldn't breathe. She stood, stumbled, pulled herself upright, then turned and began to run. In just a few seconds, the time it took her to disappear into a swarm of tourists, the world, as she had known it, was totally transformed. With the utterance of just two words, her entire life was changed. She could hear Ari calling out behind her. She couldn't trust his words now, though, no matter what he said. She shoved through the crowd and kept on running. She never wanted to see him again. She had been reduced to something ugly and foolish. All she wanted now was to vanish forever.

She ran south and then west until she reached the Hudson River. Her body refused to stop moving. She ran in and out of traffic, along the West Side Highway, not hearing the honking or the skidding of tires. She ran carelessly. She ran mindlessly. She ran to get away. She ran to escape the pain that she feared would swallow her whole.

When she finally stopped, it was sudden. She looked around. The streets were empty, and she had no idea where she was. The sun had dropped to the edge of the earth. Her body was cold. Her legs were trembling. Wrapping her arms around herself, she collapsed onto the pavement and curled up into a ball.

She lay there in a bundle until night turned into day. Then someone leaned down and whispered in her ear. "God loves you," they said. "Get up, sister. Go and do his bidding." She heard the click of metal being set down on the concrete beside her. When she opened her eyes, she saw a dented lunchbox there, and the retreating back of a lone workman. She sat up. And although her mind was still a blank, she did know one thing. She had to go home.

Betrayed, she left Ari behind in New York City and returned home to her mother.

She would find her mother's betrayal to be far worse.

When I have a terrible need of—
shall I say the word—religion,
I go out and paint the stars.
- Vincent van Gogh

CHAPTER FIVE

WHEN Poppy arrived home, she was almost unrecognizable. Her long blond hair was dark with grime and tangled in knots. Her face was sallow and lifeless.

∘∘∘

"So what do we do now?" Jewell slammed the door of the house as she and Jane headed out for their early-morning walk. Her immaculately-styled pageboy swung neatly from side to side. Jane had a blunt cut now that reached her shoulders and was easier to tend to. She was no longer as fussy as her sister about how she looked. Though both had kept their trim figures, they dressed in different styles now. Jewell preferred European fashions, while Jane was content with what she found at Wanamaker's in Philadelphia.

"Well, you can't put her in that home for unwed mothers in Bryn Mawr. Everyone sends their daughters there," Jane said, catching up.

"Well, of course I can't," Jewell shouted, leading them

up a hill and into the woods. "But what can I do. She can't keep staying here. And what about Collier? It would just be too much for him." They reached the stream they normally stopped at, and leaned against a tree to rest.

"Well then, what about that Carmelite Convent on the other side of Philadelphia? Remember, Mother used to drag us there every year to go to mass and give them a contribution. It's in such a remote place it would take her hours to find it. But she loved it there for some reason. I bet they would take in an unwed mother. Especially with Father Sean's help," Jane said. "I know he has good connections there. He'll be able to do whatever we need."

Jewell was silent for a moment.

"Well," said Jane, "what do you think of that idea?"

"I'm thinking," Jewell said sharply. "I don't know."

"The nuns will take good care of her, I'm sure," Jane assured her.

"And then what? What if she wants to keep the baby after it's born? She's too young to be caring for anyone other than herself. And she'd be doing it alone," Jewell said, as she straightened up, stepped over the stream, and kept on walking.

"Well, if she kept it we could help her," Jane said tentatively.

"That would tie her to us just when she is meant to be breaking free. I want this done, done and done. I want it over with. The nuns will arrange the adoption. They will pick out a good Catholic couple, and the whole thing will be anonymous."

Jane followed slowly behind her sister. "Yes, that would

indeed be the easy way out. But I'm sure there are other ways. After all, do we really want the baby to go to just anyone?"

Jewell stopped in her tracks. "I never thought of that. I don't know," she said.

"Well," Jane said calmly, her heart beginning to beat wildly in her chest, "we could... if you wanted... make arrangements for the baby to go to someone we know and trust."

Jewell looked up, beyond the woods, toward the horizon.

"Yes," she agreed. "We could." Her breath caught. "And if we knew who the baby was going to," she whispered, "we could follow it. That way we could make certain it was always safe."

ooo

Every morning during her first week at the convent, Poppy woke up with a start, wondering for a moment where she was. Being there felt to her like there was a hole in the world, and she had fallen into it. The walls of her room were blank, except for a crucifix that hung at the head of her bed, where her painting should have been. There was a chest of drawers that held her underclothes, socks, and sweaters. In her closet hung three dresses.

The nuns wore long white habits, and were always busy. The clicking sound of the rosary beads at their sides echoed wherever they went. They were cordial and firm, but she could tell by the looks on their faces that they judged her as morally corrupt and not worthy of the glory of Heaven.

Poppy never felt a need to speak to anyone. She kept

to herself. She blended into the walls as much as she could. At night, she wrote poems in a composition book Jane had given her. In the morning, she tore them out and threw them away.

Really, it was just her and her child there. The nuns disappeared after a while. The baby became her best friend. The source of her strength, and her hope. Because the baby was inside her, she knew she could survive anything. She talked to it all the time. She told it that the world was a wonderful place and when it was time to be born, there were things like music and colors and magic and laughter and the moon and the stars to experience. And there was love. "Love for yourself and love for someone else, and they are both equally essential. And you will have things to do in this world. Important things. That is why you are here. And there is bravery," she told her child. "We are both going to have to be very brave. Out in the world, you never know what to expect. Sometimes, a thing seems like it's going to be right, when in fact, it's not the right thing at all. Remember that. Remember that always."

∘∘∘

Poppy had weekly visitors: her mother, her aunt, and Father Sean Patrick. Her father came once, but it was such an uncomfortable place for him to be, he didn't return. There was a garden at the convent, and most Sundays, her mother, her aunt and Father Sean would walk with her. They talked and talked. And Poppy listened.

They walked through the fallen leaves in the autumn. "Are you thinking about going back to school after the baby is born?" her mother asked. "You're such a gifted writer, it would be a shame to stop your education now,"

Jane said as she put her arm around Poppy's shoulder. Father Sean, ambling behind them, added, "It seems a pity to not use the talents God gave you."

That winter the snow was high, but that did not keep them inside. "I know you want the best for this baby," Jane smiled, as she reached for Poppy's hand and kissed it. Jewell took Poppy's other hand, rubbing it warm. "A mother instinctively knows what's right for her child," she said. "The most important thing is the well-being of the child, don't you think? That's what you need to focus on," Father Sean suggested softly.

In the spring, among the daffodils, their weekly walks continued. The baby had grown bigger by then, making it more difficult for Poppy to keep up with the others. "It looks to me like you don't have long before the baby is born," Father Sean said, deliberately walking slowly with her so they could be alone. "You have to be realistic now, Poppy, about what you can give this child and what this child deserves."

Poppy listened to every single word they said. And although everyone was very careful to avoid using the word *adoption*, the idea of it was always present, floating around them, dangling between them, whenever they met. Poppy lay awake at nights, paralyzed with fear. She had no idea what to do.

A week before the baby was due, things finally came to a head. "You can't be selfish," her mother began, with a hint of irritation in her voice. "You can't just think of yourself. You're not a little girl anymore, you can't pretend that everything is going to be all right." Taking Poppy by the shoulders, she stared into her eyes. "This child needs an adult mother, an adult father, a real family to bring it up.

31

You are still a child yourself. You can't give it any of those things. In fact," she leaned in close and whispered in her ear so no one else could hear, "you have nothing to offer this baby. Nothing at all. And to think that you do, is not only greedy and reckless, but irresponsible."

Her mother's words struck Poppy like a sharp arrow through the center of her heart. For several moments she could hardly breathe. Tears flooded her eyes and spilled out and down her face. Turning abruptly, she walked away. Her mother's words had left her speechless. They were cruel and callous, and would remain with her for many years to come. It had never occurred to her that keeping her child would be greedy, reckless or irresponsible. All she wanted was for her baby to be loved. And she had so much love in her. But now, after years and years of believing in herself, she suddenly doubted everything. She doubted her own mind, she doubted her ability to take care of herself, and she certainly doubted her ability to take care of a child. She was a person standing at a crossroads, who had to choose between two impossible paths. And neither seemed bearable. The possibility of keeping her child and failing it was excruciating. The thought of giving it up was unendurable.

∞

The three magnificent flames of turquoise, sapphire and indigo blue hovered, like hummingbirds, waiting to see who would be called first. They swayed this way and that, each trembling apprehensively, craving to be the one chosen. Then the moment came.

"I am being called," the flame of sapphire proclaimed, tingling with delight. Then, dissolving into a wisp of smoke, paused for a moment, swirled a grand farewell, and crossed over the great divide.

∞

Poppy got to see her daughter once, for less than five minutes, on April 19th, the day of her birth. They were in the small hospital where she'd been rushed to give birth. And even though her child was across the room, five feet away, and the lights were dim, she could see the baby's eyes were big and brown just like Ari's. She also saw that her baby had a distinctive mark above her heart. A birthmark in the shape of a crescent moon. When asked to fill out her baby's name on the birth certificate, she wrote, Luna Russell Doumas. She knew this was the last time she would ever see her daughter.

"Remember when I told you about love? Well, real love is when the other person's happiness is more important than your own. And there is nothing more important to me than your happiness, my little Luna."

She had decided to do something that even in the doing felt impossible.

She covered her face and began to sob.

°°°

"I can't believe it," Jane said, after the doctor left her and Father Sean alone in the waiting room. Tears welled up in her eyes and she quickly wiped them away. Jewell was still in with Poppy, who was crying uncontrollably after seeing her baby for the first and last time. Neither one had been present when the doctor had come to inform them that the baby Poppy had given birth to had a serious heart murmur.

"I cannot, in good conscience, give my nephew and his wife a baby with health problems," said Father Sean. "The care she might need could put them in financial jeopardy. And they've wanted a baby for so long, they deserve to have one born without problems."

Jane put her head in her hands. Everything had been so carefully planned, and now it was all unraveling. If the baby didn't go with Father Sean's relatives, then they would lose contact with her entirely. Their plans of following the baby through her life would be thrown out the window. And if Jewell couldn't watch her granddaughter grow up, she would surely let Poppy keep the little girl after all. And Poppy's future would be decided, her life ruined.

Jane drew herself up and took a deep breath. No, she thought to herself. *I won't let that happen*. Whatever she had to do, she had to keep that from ever happening.

"This is a small hospital," she began. "It'll be easy to do. I'm going to switch Poppy's baby with a healthy one," she whispered to Father Sean. "I'll just switch the wristbands and do something with the birthmark. Fitz knows a lot of doctors. I am certain one can help. Whatever needs to be done, Father, I will do it." she said. She waited for his response, impatiently. "This way, you can give your nephew a perfect child. And Jewell will have a baby to follow who she thinks is her granddaughter," she added.

Father Sean sat in silence, unmoving. Jane waited impatiently for him to respond.

"What do you think, Father? Do you have another loving family who wants to adopt a child with the means to care for Poppy's real baby?"

Father Sean blessed himself. "Yes," he answered quietly.

The foot feels the foot
when it feels the ground.
- Buddha

CHAPTER SIX

IT WAS past midnight when, a week after giving birth, Poppy left the farm she had lived on all her life without a word to anyone. She took essentials and her picture of the church in Paris, so the green plaid suitcase she carried would not be too heavy. She didn't know exactly where she was going, but she did know that she was never coming back. It was seven country miles to the Paoli train station, and by the time she reached it, she was damp all over with fresh spots of silvery dew. An early morning train was just about to leave. She had one hundred dollars in her purse.

She bought a one-way ticket, boarded quickly, and took a seat beside the window. She watched as towns like Devon, Villanova, Bryn Mawr and Haverford flew past, disappearing behind her. The further away she got, the easier it was for her to breathe. At one point, she noticed a reflection in the window. It wasn't until she tilted her head back and forth a few times that she realized it was her own. In the reflection she looked surer somehow, braver, bolder. As the train sped on, passing buildings, trees, a grassy, green park, a little boy with a dragon kite tucked under his arm, an advertising blimp just rising up into the sky, she sensed that a fog was gently lifting from her. It was as though she was, in some way, a despairing wild animal who had unexpectedly been let out of its cage and was finally, marvelously free.

It was then, without much thought, that she took out a pen and notebook from her bag, and began to write. She didn't waver, not once. The words just poured out of her like fresh spring water flows from a shiny new spigot. And as she wrote, she was bewildered to find that, unlike anything she'd written before, she was writing a children's story. A tale, a fairy tale really, set in an entirely different world. The story came out of her and shaped itself as quickly as her pen could move.

LUNA

"What a lovely little child," passersby would murmur behind gloved hands, when her governess would stroll with her through the park in her navy blue carriage on Sunday afternoons. No little baby they had ever seen before was so strikingly beautiful and delicate. Her gleaming locks seemed spun from gold, her skin soft as rain, and her small, gentle face was so kindly that only the most merciless soul didn't melt in awe of it. And because she had a birthmark in the shape of a crescent moon over her heart, she had been named Luna.

The governess was a battle-axe of a woman who dressed all in white from head to toe. She was so hardhearted that she barely touched Baby Luna or allowed anyone else to, not even her mother. "Holding the infant can produce neediness, you know. Let them cry if they must," she said. "It's good for their lungs and gives them strength of character."

Luna did indeed have great strength of character, as she cried at the top of her lungs without stopping for the first six months of her life. This was, of course, very annoying, but paled in comparison, in her governess's humble view, to the real crux of the child's problems. What disquieted her the most and caused her a large amount of unrest was a certain extraordinary, otherworldly ability the infant possessed. The baby could levitate, and did so regularly, even slipping out of the open nursery window, at the age of three months, almost escaping, until the governess—always vigilant—grabbed a tiny ankle just in time and pulled her back in.

Fearful of reporting this incident to the child's parents, as it might cause her to lose her position, she decided instead to take care of the matter herself. She devised a way to fasten her small charge's wrists to the sides of her crib and carriage with golden chains, to keep her from getting away again.

Baby Luna, just a few days old when she had been put in the care of her governess, had recognized all along that she was being mistreated, and she didn't like it. Not one bit.

I'm not having any more of this, she decided, after a few months passed. *I might be a baby*, she determined, as she lay in her cradle un-rocked and un-touched and chained to the sides, *I might be incapable of expressing my opinions so they can be understood*, she reasoned as she cried loudly and beat her little feet in the air, *I might even be small and defenseless*, she deduced as she struggled to catch her breath in between sobs, *but I do have a very sharp mind, and I am very clever. Therefore, I must have the capacity to solve this predicament.*

Searching her brain for a practical solution, it came to her finally one afternoon when she was on the verge of turning one year old. She was on an outing, in the park, chained in her carriage, being pushed by her atrocious governess, when the sight of a very flamboyant dragon kite, in flight above her, caused her to recall the short flight she'd attempted to take from the nursery window, some time back. *I can do that*, she said to herself. *I did do that. And I will do it again*, she determined. Then, without hesitation, without a thought to the consequences of what she was doing, she gathered all of her authority, her strength, and her power, and snapped the glittering, golden chains that had held her in place for so long. Smiling gloriously, she began to rise.

"Come here at once," the governess bellowed, jumping up in an attempt to grab Luna's tiny silken shoe. But alas, she was seconds too late. Levitating herself just inches out of reach, Luna hovered there, taunting and teasing, until her governess's face turned so scarlet that it looked as though it was a boiling bubble about to explode.

And Luna rose further and further up into the air, through the puffy white cumulus clouds, and evaporated out of sight. The higher she rose, the older she got. She could sense her body transforming as she soared further and further away from Earth. By the time she reached her destination, she was no longer a baby, but a little girl.

"My baby. My baby," Luna's young mother wept when she received the report that Luna had vanished into thin air. For although she had not once been permitted to hold her sweet darling daughter, smell her dear golden head, tickle her soft belly and cause her to laugh, she nevertheless loved and adored her. The news of Luna's disappearance thus broke her heart and she would never, ever, be the same again.

∘∘∘

Several hours later, when Poppy felt the train jerk to a stop, she looked up, startled. She had been so immersed in the world of Luna, it took her a moment to adjust to finding herself at Penn Station in New York City. She packed up the notebook she'd been writing in, got off the train and, when she exited the dark station, the bright, blazing sun shone down on her, and she reached up to shade her eyes. It was still morning. People rushed by her on the streets, pushing her aside. She didn't mind being alone. In fact, she liked it that way. Within an hour, she'd found a room at the YWCA, and within a week she'd found a job as a bookstore clerk, and begun a brand new life.

∘∘∘

As much as she tried to rid herself of it by walking intensely mile after mile, over the Brooklyn Bridge and back, through lower and upper Manhattan, from the Hudson River to the East River, from Queens all the way to Yonkers, the pain and longing for her child followed her like a relentless shadow. Every cry from a baby she heard left her choking back sobs. She turned away when a carriage or a stroller went by. She would go out of her way to avoid playgrounds and schools and couples with young children. Another compulsion, a command she gave herself, was never to accept a single hint of Ari into her thoughts, for she recognized that would extinguish her entirely.

Completely alone in the world, she didn't have anyone around to notice exactly when her preoccupation with order and control began. Slowly, little by little, day-by-day, it became more and more important to her to have things her way. Every object she encountered had to be aligned with everything around it. This worked to her advantage in the bookstore, where alphabetizing and shelving books were part of her duties, but it did not endear her to her colleagues when she began redoing their work. What also took hold was a feeling of overpowering guilt for not being strong enough to keep her baby. Drawing up lists of all her life's other wrongdoings, she came up with a strategy to redeem herself. This plan involved her giving away her gold class ring to a stranger on the subway who happened to admire it; secretly slipping the tortoiseshell barrette that once belonged to her grandmother into the handbag of an unsuspecting customer; and silently handing over her camel's hair coat to a homeless woman she passed by on a corner. But no matter what Poppy did, no matter what she gave away, it was never enough. Her hands always felt dirty, as though they were covered in a sticky slime she couldn't get rid of. Poppy washed and scrubbed them hard every chance she got with a coarse soap she carried in a plastic container. They began to swell and crack and turn so red that she was compelled to wear gloves in order to hide them.

One day, Poppy noticed they were bleeding. The sight of the blood so startled her she could barely breathe. The shorter and quicker her breaths got, the more frightened she became. What had she done to herself? What was happening to her? Was she going mad? A great black wave rose from within her. A silent scream.

It was then that Poppy understood she couldn't trust herself to do what was in her best interest. She knew she had to ask for help. And the first place she went was to St. Patrick's Cathedral. She lit a candle in front of the statue of St. Anthony, the patron saint of lost things. "Please," she prayed, "help me find peace."

ooo

It was at this time that she remembered the chapter she'd written on the train ride to New York. She searched for the notebook in all of her drawers, in her closet, and under the bed. That's when she saw her suitcase. In the inside pocket of the lid, waiting patiently for her all this time, were the first words she'd written about Luna. She read through it, and then she continued to write. She wrote in coffee shops and the 42nd Street Library, at work and at the laundromat. Wherever she could, she wrote. She never planned what she was going to write. She just allowed it to pour out of her. Luna's world was the only comfort she had, and she wanted to be nowhere else. When it began to get cold, she wrote on the subway because it was always warm there. Mostly, she rode the RR train that went from Queens all the way to Coney Island. She just went back and forth, for hours on end. One day, she looked up from her pages and there was Ari Doumas. Standing right in front of her.

He was just there, his hands in his pockets, staring down at her. He was wearing faded jeans and an old striped shirt with the sleeves rolled up. His dark hair was long now and fell to his shoulders. His face was leaner, his cheekbones sharper. But his eyes were the same intense brown, filled with the same passion and eagerness for life that they had always had. Suddenly she felt a sensation of love rush through her. It was so alarmingly forceful that the intensity of it took her breath away. A gasp emitted from her open mouth, which was loud enough to cause people nearby to turn and look. Mortified, her instinct was to pull herself up from the seat, push her way to the doors, and get off at the next stop. But she could not force her eyes to leave his. So she sat there, frozen in place, and her heart, her silly, impetuous heart, she thought, her unruly, willful heart, began burning away at all the wounds, the scars, the damage within her, as she and Ari silently stared at one another.

∘∘∘

"The first time I called, your mother told me that you weren't pregnant, after all," Ari told Poppy. They had gotten off the subway at the first stop they could and headed to the nearest coffee shop. "The second time I called, she said you'd fallen in love with someone else and wanted nothing to do with me. At first, I didn't want to believe it. I couldn't. I called many times after that, and each time she told me not to call again. You were getting married and going on your honeymoon, she said. I came to your house, and when she opened the door she said she would call the police if I didn't leave immediately. After that, when she'd hear my voice on the phone, because I kept calling, she would just hang up on me," he told her. "I really was separated from my wife when you and I were together," he said, reaching for her hand. "It was an arranged marriage. She'd come over from Greece. I hardly even knew her. I didn't tell you because I was afraid it would unnecessarily complicate things, and it was so early in our relationship. But I was wrong. I should have told you right from the start. I should have told you that a week after you and I met I filed for divorce."

"We do have a baby, Ari. And she looks so much like you. I named her Luna. And I had to give her up for adoption. I think about her every waking moment," Poppy told him, tears running down her face. "I never even got to hold her." Ari stared at her in disbelief. He tried to speak, to say something, anything. No words came. He put his face in his hands, and as he cried, his entire body trembled with grief.

They were never apart again after that meeting on the subway. They would spend the next months mourning the loss of their daughter and the life they could have had with her. Slowly, carefully, Poppy began to learn to trust again. As they grew closer, Ari did all he could to repair the damage that had been done.

Together, they resolved to shape a new life.

∘ ∘ ∘

A year after Luna's birth, Poppy and Ari were married, and Poppy Russell became Poppy Russell Doumas. They were dirt poor. They found a tiny studio apartment on the Upper West Side, in a sixth-floor walk-up. It consisted of a stove with two burners and an oven you couldn't fit a turkey into. Their first purchase was a second-hand Castro convertible couch, which the Super and his burly son helped them carry up all those flights of stairs. They had a card table, where Poppy's second-hand portable Remington typewriter sat, with mismatched chairs they found discarded on the street; a bookshelf made out of bricks and wooden planks from a construction site for all of Ari's books; and Poppy's painting of the church with a single steeple. They were proud of their small apartment and all of its treasures. Especially the Steuben vase Ari's boss had given them as a wedding present, which they filled with flowers Ari brought home from the local flower shop at half price every Saturday night. Most importantly, they finally had each other.

Poppy loved to sit on the edge of the bathtub in their cramped bathroom and watch Ari shave, a towel wrapped around his waist. It was her favorite part of the day. Each morning, she was able to see and hear the power of each masterful stroke as the razor glided down his face, so that when he was finally finished and leaned over to her, she could place the palm of her hand on his smooth skin, knowing that he was really hers. This everyday, simple occurrence would be something she would cherish for the rest of her life.

And Ari's love was a salve. Each time Poppy was in danger of being swallowed up once more in guilt, and just as she was on the verge of resorting to washing her hands and aligning everything in the house, Ari was right there by her side, soothing her, comforting her, showing her with his whole being that she was worthy of being loved. And he always encouraged her to continue writing about Luna.

Before you found me I was lingering on the edge, waiting to die, Poppy wrote to Ari on their first anniversary. *You have rekindled my desire to live.*

Every new beginning comes
from some other beginning's end.
- Seneca

CHAPTER SEVEN

THE YEAR was 1347. Just as Eustache de Saint Pierre was leaving home, he felt a small cobblestone come loose from the street in front of the grand manor in which he lived. He rolled it back and forth under the sole of his sandal for a moment, and then, bending down, he picked it up and rolled it again between his thumb and forefinger. Its oblong body was smooth and warm and soothing to him, and he wondered how many thousands in his war-torn town of Calais had passed along this street, and had trod upon this same stone, before it loosened and became free. He lifted his head toward the warmth of the morning sun. This would be the last time he would feel its heat. This would be the last time he would see its glow reflected off the leaves of the few olive trees around that had survived the most recent drought. This would also be the last time, he knew, that he would shield his eyes from it as he looked up toward where his dear wife, Marian, stood at the window of their bedroom, her quivering hands held over her mouth in an attempt to force back the cries of anguish she held courageously within.

Eustache de Saint Pierre was one of the wealthiest of

the town leaders. That is what King Edward III of England had demanded: six volunteers, all noblemen, or *burghers*, to surrender themselves to him for execution. The king, who the year before had laid siege to the important French port between England and France, had also commanded that the six men wear nooses around their necks, and carry the keys to the city in their hands. In exchange, Edward III would spare the starving people of Calais. Thus, Eustache, his heart aching for the thousands left dying and dead in the streets, had offered himself up. He had been the very first to do so. Soon after, five other *burghers* had joined him. They were to present themselves outside the city gates that day, where, before noon, their lives would be ended.

Eustache continued to roll the smooth cobblestone between his fingers. It was an unassuming stone. An ordinary stone. But it was to be, by simple chance, the only possession he would have when he left this world. And though it was just a common object, it was now as valuable to him as a nugget of gold, not only because of its earthliness, but because he could hold it unseen. With the stone buried in his clenched fist, he turned and stepped out of the sun and away, far away, from the sweet face of his wife, who watched after him until he gradually disappeared from sight.

° ° °

In 1884, the city of Calais would commission one of the most famous sculptors, Auguste Rodin, to create *The Burghers of Calais*. Rodin was able to capture in bronze, the six brave men who had offered their lives that day, five-hundred years before. This sculpture would stand in twelve different cities years later, including Calais, and the

46

Rodin Museum in Paris. After Eustache and the others offered to make the ultimate sacrifice, Edward III's wife, Philippa, became scared that their execution might curse the heir she carried in her womb. She begged her husband to relent and spare their lives. And thus, Eustache de Saint Pierre would die not at the gates of Calais with five others, as crowds watched on, but instead in his own bed many years later, with only Marian nearby.

But Eustache would not pass into the next world entirely content. For although Marian still loved him and continued to tell him so often since the day he had been set free by Edward III, he had detected a change in her toward him. She was not at the door to their home when he'd returned. Nor could he find her after he had pushed his way through the crowds of people that had gathered to welcome him and sing his praises. When he finally did locate her it was in the kitchen, hidden among the cooks. She had not expected him until evening, she told him, and she had been busy supervising a splendid feast for him upon his return. Before Eustache had left to martyr himself for his town, Marian had always been full of gladness and delight. She had laughed at even his most trivial of tales, and let herself be disrobed when he requested, at night, under the radiance of candles. But now, since his return, a melancholy had set in. This mirthlessness not only darkened her heart, but also, after a time, dimmed his as well. As days grew into weeks and then months, her reclusiveness became more and more evident.

After that, all the praise bestowed upon him by people who came to visit from near and far, began to feel inconsequential and undeserving. He did not understand it. He pleaded with her to tell him what it was that troubled her so. He beseeched her to spend time with him and let him, at the very least, hold her soft hand. But all his imploring came to no avail. The despondency in his wife left him confused and muddled. He had believed his decision to offer his life in exchange for the safety of his city had been a noble act; that his motives had been altruistic. But now, knowing his wife to be a reasonable woman, whose disposition could be trusted and relied upon, he began to doubt and question himself. If his wife was not proud of him, as all others were, then most likely he had not acted nobly at all. And if this was true, then the offer of his life in exchange for the safety of his town, had not been magnanimous at all, but greedy and selfish and, he determined in the still of one moonless night, merely a way for him to quench his craving to be a hero and a champion—a secret fantasy that he had harbored most of his life. Furthermore, he reasoned, by ensuring that his name go down in history, he had abandoned Marian, his dear and faithful Marian, to care and fend for herself. Embarrassed by the man he began to think he was, he avoided his friends and began to seclude himself in his room.

His only solace during this time was the small stone he had kept from that day. Staring out the window, he would roll the well-worn cobblestone between his fingers, feeling the wholeness of it. Because it was so modest, so humble, and came from the earth, it brought comfort to him.

As time passed, his house became a premature tomb; hushed, still and silent, filled with unspoken thoughts and buried emotions. If only he had it to do over again, he wished as he sat alone by his window. If only he had turned back to Marian that day as she stood by the window looking down at him. If only he had come back home to her that morning, instead of going to the gates of Calais. A useless act, as it turned out, an act of a dreamer, an idealist, a romantic with delusions of grandeur. The frustration of remembering it all made him weak at the knees. Just as he was reaching for the stone, he fell across his bed. *If only*, he implored the heavens above before he took his final breath, *I could live my life again and make it all right.*

In the beginning, he detected the absence of conflict. He spread his arms and found that all restraints had disappeared. A profound sense of peace surged through him. He swirled through a tunnel of dazzling light, and over a bridge. On the other side, he felt himself soften into the morning mist. As he glided by the past, the present, and the yet-to-be, he understood he was home again. It was then that he began his hum.

Franklyn Doyle, born in 1940, was the middle child in a family three generations out of Ireland. He grew up in a noisy home, and the only peace he ever found was at Old Saint Joseph's, the oldest church in Philadelphia, where he was an altar boy. The Catholic faith was a big part of his life and that of his family. His mother's brother, Sean Patrick, in fact, was a priest.

Franklyn was a good student. His main interest in life, however, was collecting stones. His friends all called him

RH, which stood for Rock Hound. When he graduated high school he went to Temple University, where he became a geologist. It was there that he met Nellie, who was studying to be a nurse. They fell head-over-heels in love with each other, and were married within a few months. Though they wanted to have children right away, years passed, and they weren't able to conceive. Until a miracle happened, and their prayers for a baby were answered.

When Franklyn took the small bundle that the nurse in white handed him, tears of joy rolled down his face. "She is beautiful," he said, smiling at his wife. "She is the most beautiful baby I have seen in my life."

∘∘∘

Kate Doyle was born with what felt like a missing piece in her soul, despite the overwhelming love her parents showered her with daily. She was the most amazing little creature they had ever set eyes on, and they cherished her beyond reason. Especially her father, who was a gentle man, a man whose love for his wife and his daughter would always take precedence over everything else in his life. His feelings for his family came from deep in his soul and permeated everything he did. Before little Kate had turned three, he had taught his daughter the names of all the different types of plants he had introduced over the years into his sunny garden at the back of their small, white stucco home. The garden was a mixture of plants, flowers, and stones. Stones of all shapes, that he and Kate collected on walks along a nearby beach, were incorporated into the winding paths through it all. "Just think, Kate," he told her one day as they were walking barefooted along the ocean's edge. "That very stone in your hand is a part of history.

50

Who knows how long it's been here." "I think it's been here a long time," she responded.

° ° °

On Kate's first day of school, she donned her new plaid uniform and walked into her classroom at St. Anne's School. It was just three short blocks from their new home on an island off Florida's East Coast. She already knew how to read and write. In fact, she had been reading to herself and writing paragraphs since she was four. But that did not stop her from being overwhelmed like all the other children in first grade that day. From the moment she set eyes on her teacher, Sister Teresa, who was dressed in a black habit and long white veil, Kate felt a fiery yearning that made her sweet face turn pink and her six-year-old heart beat fast. Sister Teresa's smile was radiant. She seemed filled with a peace that even some of the first grade boys couldn't shatter. She read to them every day from *The Book of Saints*. She was perfect in every way. *I want to be like Sister Teresa*, Kate thought. *I want to wear a long veil and habit. I want to be a nun someday*. This, Kate decided, could be the answer to what was missing inside her.

February 17, 1971
Dear St. Bernadette,

I hope it's ok that I am writing to you. I am better at writing than reciting prayers. Sister Teresa read a story about you today to our class and I just want you to know that you are my favorite Saint.

Your friend,
Kate Doyle

Mary Ellen McCormack was the biggest thorn in Kate's side her first year at St. Anne's. A day did not pass that Mary Ellen wasn't waiting for her at the front door of the school when Kate arrived in the morning, having been walked the few blocks from her home by her beautiful, dark-haired mother. The undersized girl with freckles covering her entire body seemed smitten— with Kate, and especially with the mark of a crescent moon that Kate had just above her heart.

"Can I touch it?" Mary Ellen worked up her nerve to ask one day, her finger poised. "No, you cannot," Kate told her. "My mother says it's never to be touched by anyone but her and me and my father. It's sacred. I'm holy, you know. It's a mark of holiness. It's a secret now, so you can't breathe a word about it, but some day I will be entering the church as a nun. Most probably I'll become a saint, that's why I've been given the mark. You may be praying to me, lighting candles to me some day. So you better stop following me around or I may not grant you your requests."

October 22, 1972
Dear Saint Bernadette,

Sister Teresa said that God gives us friends and sometimes we don't know why. We just have to be accepting and tolerant. I certainly wish that He had given me someone else less exasperating than Mary Ellen.

Your friend,
Kate Doyle

Mary Ellen believed what Kate told her. There was no doubt in her mind that her friend was holy. Kate was constantly on her knees praying. She was continually talking about God, the Virgin Mary, and her favorite saint, Bernadette. Just a few days ago, in fact, the strangest thing had happened. Two women who looked like each other had approached Kate and asked to have their picture taken with her. They had a Polaroid camera and took two, giving the second one to Kate. Kate didn't seem to find this strange; she just put it in her school bag and walked away to class. The women looked at her as though she had a halo over her head. Mary Ellen wondered if maybe there really was one, and she just couldn't see it.

Whenever they were alone, Kate would drape a white sheet around her head, letting it fall down her shoulders and her back, all the way to the floor. "Mary Ellen?" she would say. "Do I look like a nun? Do you see my knees?" she would ask. "They are nuns' knees because they are red and swollen from praying." Mary Ellen crossed her heart and hoped to die if she ever told anyone Kate's secret of wanting to become a nun. Nevertheless, she could not keep herself from following her around, which she did until the day the two of them graduated school years later. It was a good thing she did remain a loyal friend, because Kate desperately needed Mary Ellen's presence during that time.

Kate's mother left home suddenly when she was in the middle of third grade. "Where did she go?" she asked. "I don't know," her father answered. "When will she be back?" she asked. "I don't know," he said again, "maybe when she finds what she's off looking for."

So Kate waited. Night and day, she wondered what it was that her mother was out there looking for and when she found it, would she come home again? Each morning she opened her eyes and thought that maybe today was the day... maybe today was the day she would be there for breakfast.

Out of suffering have emerged
the strongest souls.
The most massive characters
are seared with scars.
- Khalil Gibran

CHAPTER EIGHT

ONE DAY at the end of fourth grade, Kate's father sat her down in the living room that they never used, so Kate knew it would be an important conversation. He told her that he and her mother had gotten a matrimonial dispensation from the Pope in Rome, Italy, and that their marriage was dissolved. "Kind of like a snowball dissolving when it gets too hot?" Kate asked. "Exactly," her father said, turning away with tears in his eyes. Kate saw the tears and knew her father was very sad. All this time he had made it seem like he was doing okay. And she saw now that he was sad in the same way that she was sad. And more than anything she wanted to make him happy again. So from that day on, she would comfort him whenever she could. She held his hand a lot more when they went on walks together and let him pick out clothes for her she didn't really like. His sadness continued to make her sad though, no matter what. "Where did she go?" she asked him again when he was tucking her into bed one night. "I don't know. She always talked about wanting to live in Paris, France," he told her. "Maybe she is there."

°°°

Mary Ellen convinced Kate to join the track team, where Kate learned to run like the wind. But no matter how hard she ran, she couldn't run away from how she felt inside sometimes. One day, when Kate was in sixth grade, she cut all her long dark hair off. She had found herself daydreaming about how her mother used to brush it and say how beautiful it was. *So why did she leave me if my hair was so beautiful?* And she took a pair of scissors to it. When she was finished there was a pile of locks on the floor and her almost naked head was sharp with inch-long hair. Later, embarrassed to confess the truth, she told Mary Ellen that what she had done was in preparation for becoming a nun. In solidarity, Mary Ellen cut off her own long hair. And together, side-by-side, they prayed daily.

That was the summer Mary Ellen and Kate discovered the *Luna* series by P.R. Doumas. Mary Ellen had found them in the library and taken out the two books published so far, mainly because the main character had a birthmark shaped just like Kate's, in the very same spot. "I hope she never stops writing them," Kate announced after she had devoured them. "I feel like they were written just for me." She laughed, knowing it was impossible, but wishing it were true. "I know exactly what you mean," Mary Ellen agreed. And, wanting desperately to be just like Kate and Luna, Mary Ellen took to drawing crescent moons over her heart with a pen—much like half the world's young readers, who had the same idea. It wasn't unusual, in summertime, to see gaggles of girls with crescent moons emblazoned over *their* hearts.

Inspired by one of their favorite stories of the series so far, Mary Ellen and Kate, as most other children around the world, played endless games that summer of what they called War and Peace.

∘∘∘

LUNA AND THE REVERSALS

"Welcome. We have been waiting for you," the tall, slim girl said. She was holding out her hands. She had a heavy dark braid falling down her back and a mark in the shape of a teardrop under her right eye. She was beautiful, Luna thought, regal, like an empress of some kind.

Looking around, Luna saw smooth, round mounds, each with a small opening in the front. There were hundreds of them, all a soft orange hue, the same shade as the ground. Behind the mounds, blending in so well that it was difficult to detect at first, was a high wall with what looked like diamonds encrusted across the top. This was not what Luna had imagined the moon would look like.

The dark-haired girl clapped her hands together and abruptly hundreds of girls of all ages, heights and colors, came out from the mounds and timidly began to approach, surrounding her. They wore tunics the same orange hue as the ground, the mounds and the wall, tied with cords, from which hung sheaths. Luna marveled at the fact that though they all seemed to come out at the same time, none of them made a single sound. They were like inaudible orange puffs of vapor slipping through the light.

The dark-haired girl lifted her arm and together they all obediently lowered their heads, bowing to Luna on bended knees.

"Princess Luna," they all sang out in sweet-young-girl voices. "Finally you have come to defend us." Then, a golden crown, light as a feather and a perfect fit, was set upon her head.

Luna was startled. She looked around at them—their round, wide, trusting eyes, each fixed on her and filled with hope. "I am afraid you have it all wrong. You have made some kind of mistake. I am not a princess," she called out to them. "I am just a girl," Luna said. She was so overwhelmed, all she wanted to do was levitate away. And she tried. She tried with all her might, and, after trying and failing every way she could think of to lift off, she found that her power had vanished. How would she ever return home?

Before Luna could bemoan her fate further, a thunderous roar exploded from beyond the wall.

"I'm afraid there's no time to be dithering about," the dark-haired girl called as the ground began to reverberate beneath their feet. "The Reversals have sensed your arrival and they are coming."

"The Reversals?" Luna questioned as the deafening roar came closer. "What are they?"

"You have a crescent over your heart, do you not?" the girl spoke quickly.

Luna nodded.

"Your Reversal's crescent is not over *her* heart. Her crescent is on the opposite side. That makes you the dominant and most powerful one here. She's come to destroy you," the girl rushed on. "She needs to eliminate you, seize your power, so she can take over and reign in the light, forcing us to live on the dark side of the moon."

Then, before Luna knew what was happening, she saw hundreds of dark, filthy creatures dressed in threadbare cloth, streaming over the high wall with long jagged shards held high in the air.

That is when Luna first set eyes on a girl leading the multitudes and, unexpectedly, their blue and brown eyes met one another. They were two armies of twins, mirror twins, each the reverse of the other.

And they fought. Their weapons clashed. The sky was filled with cries of anguish, torment and suffering.

It was Luna who finally brought it all to a halt. "You must make a choice. Peace or war. Choose peace and we will be united. Choose war, and we will all be destroyed and there will be nothing. I," said Luna, "choose peace."

"War," screamed the Reversals.

"Yes, war!" echoed the dark-haired girl and her followers.

And then, abruptly, there was nothing.

As quickly as they had come, they all disappeared.

The hundreds of soft, orange mounds vanished and the diamond-encrusted wall vanished, too.

And Luna stood on the moon, alone, amid the vast emptiness all around her.

ooo

The summer Kate discovered the *Luna* series was the same summer the blood in her palms appeared for the first time. It began with a wart in the palm of her left hand. She picked it and picked it until it bled. And then a strong itching developed in the palm of her right hand. Not too much later, she was bleeding from that hand, also. She showed her two bloody palms to Mary Ellen, who immediately knelt down in front of her and made the sign of the cross.

August 4, 1974
Dear Saint Bernadette,

I have stigmata. I am so filled with joy. Does this mean that I am holy like you? Should I wear gloves?

Sincerely,
Kate Doyle

One day, when her father was late coming home from work, and she was all alone with nothing to do, Kate decided to entertain herself by going through some boxes in his closet stored on a high shelf. In one of the boxes she found an old piece of paper. It was a birth certificate and it had the date of her birth on it. But her father was not listed as her father and her mother was not listed as her mother. The names on the paper were of complete strangers. Kate had read a book the year before about a boy who was adopted. She had loved the book and it had touched her deeply.

She showed the paper to her father when he got home that night. "Am I adopted?" she asked him. "No," he told her in no uncertain terms. "This paper has nothing to do with you, Kate. This is something that belongs to your mother. She forgot to take it when she went away." Because she loved her father and wanted more than anything to believe him, she wiped away her brimming tears and tried desperately not to listen to the voice deep inside that asked, *could this possibly be true? Could this be the missing piece?*

March 1, 1975
Dear Saint Bernadette,

I may not be who I think I am. I am... no one. The only person I told was Mary Ellen. She doesn't think the paper I found meant anything about me. She is a good and faithful friend so I am going to listen to what she says. But please help me. Please make my mind clear.

The strangest thing happened at the supermarket today. I saw two women who looked like twins. Except they were really old. It made me laugh to see two old women dressed almost exactly alike. I wanted to get closer to them but they turned away real fast and disappeared. I think I have seen them before someplace. Are they my guardian angels?

Please confirm.
Kate

"I have prayed about this, and I want you to know I

have a vocation," she announced to Sister Teresa one day. "I really don't think that I should wait to become a nun until after I graduate school. I think I should do it now." Sister Teresa smiled her radiant smile. "I know times have been hard for you since your mother went away, dear Kate," she said, placing her hand softly on Kate's shoulder. "Our Lord works in mysterious ways. He definitely has plans for you. Though you are young still, you have the strength of someone beyond your years. Trust in the Lord. Trust in yourself. Trust that all will be as it should be, one day soon."

∘∘∘

When she was seventeen, Kate met a boy and his dog. They went to the movies and held hands and sat on the beach and kissed. Scott Kennedy was handsome and sensitive, and an aspiring photographer of great skill. The dog was a chocolate Lab named Jude. Kate had never had a boyfriend before. But Mary Ellen had, and told her she thought Scott was cool. Her feelings confused Kate greatly, as she had been waiting all her life to enter the convent, and had planned to finally do so later that year. One night, Scott sang her a song called *Time is Time*. "Last night I looked inside the moon. And I knew you were real. So every time I look at you, you know exactly how I feel."

April 13, 1982
Dear Bernadette,

My mind says no. But my heart is overflowing with love. He makes me feel important. He gives so much meaning to my life.

I am so happy, Bernadette, so happily in love. I don't know why this is happening to me. I have promised myself to God. I am so frightened of going to hell.

Kate

ooo

Life took yet another turn when Kate's father lost his position as a geologist due to severe cutbacks at his company, and was forced to take on other jobs, one of them as a janitor. Kate helped out by getting a job herself, selling shoes. She was so good at it that she was able not only to contribute half of the rent for the tiny apartment they had to move to, but also to save a small amount each week for herself.

Over the following year, Kate's love for Scott grew stronger, as did his for her. But her desire to join the religious life and become a bride of Christ was equally strong. Torn in half, Kate had a decision to make. Would she become a postulant—live and work with other Sisters for a year, then take her vows and become a nun—as she had dreamed of doing for most of her life? Or, would she stay in the secular world and continue being with Scott?

"You must pray on this, my dear," Sister Teresa advised. "Ask for guidance. Be in the world alone for a while. Take some time, away, by yourself."

February 20, 1983
Dear Bernadette,

My heart aches more and more each day. My world is falling apart. I pray to you please, help me.

K

Using the money she'd saved, she traveled to Rome, where she received a blessing from the Pope. This she found quite ironic, as it was the Pope who had blessed the dissolution of her parents' marriage years before. Then she went on to Lourdes, where, for two weeks, she stayed in a hostel for pilgrims, praying daily in front of the cave-grotto of St. Bernadette. In the end, however, despite all her prayers and supplications, she was still uncertain as to what she should do. Feeling totally hopeless, she wept into her hands, at the foot of the statue of St. Bernadette, where so many miracles had occurred. "Please don't give up on me," she beseeched. "Help me find my way."

Start by doing what is necessary,
then do what is possible,
and suddenly you are doing the impossible.
- Francis of Assisi

CHAPTER NINE

SHE WAS the smallest thing Franklyn had ever seen. Of course, he had never been close to a baby before. He had seen them in passing, at the grocery store, on the bus, and in elevators, where once a baby cried so loudly he had to get off five floors too soon. Though he and Nellie had been trying to have children for a long time now, a baby of his own was still such an abstract concept.

That changed the moment their daughter was placed in his arms.

Right from the start, baby Kate trusted him. Like nobody else in the world had ever done. The feeling that this creature's entire life was in his hands was unlike anything he had ever experienced before. The unconditional love he felt for her was immediate and overwhelming—as was the absolute terror. Terror that she would come to harm, terror that she might be taken away from him, terror that he would fail her.

At night, when his wife and daughter were both asleep,

he would lie awake, protecting them. He would listen to the steady sound of Kate's breathing. If she hesitated for half a second, he would hold his own breath, so he could hear better when she finally exhaled. She made little noises in her sleep, little squeaks and groans. If Nellie didn't wake up and beg him to get some sleep, he probably would have remained awake the whole first year of Kate's life.

∘∘∘

The first night after Nellie left them and Kate was asleep, Franklyn sat alone in their bedroom. He sat in the chair by the window all night long. He heard the dog bark, three houses down. The neighbors left him in the backyard day and night for protection.

"As if there is some kind of danger around here," Nellie used to say, laughing. "This is probably the safest street in Florida. Nothing bad happens here. In fact nothing at all happens here, ever."

He thought of those words as he rocked in the chair. They were the first hint she had given him of her discontent. But he had not really heard them. He thought about how she smelled of fresh gardenias. He thought about the way she pressed her lips together when she was thinking. He thought about her hair and how it shimmered in the sunlight.

How could he have been so blind to Nellie's unhappiness. Slowly, the woman he had loved so dearly had turned into someone else. She became distant, uninterested, and then totally taken up with going back to school. Little by little she no longer had time for him or Kate or anything at home. Beds were left unmade,

66

dishes and clothes were unwashed, counter tops and floors were grimy with filth, and the only food in the house was food he had shopped for on his way home from work. She had left them one rainy spring day when Kate was in school and he was at work. "I want more out of life than just stability," her note had said. "I need to be a part of a larger world."

He didn't understand how their marriage had fallen apart like that, and he never would. They had been so happy, the three of them. At least he had thought they had been. Where had she gone, he wondered. She had always talked of living in Paris. He would have taken her to Paris. He would have done anything to have kept her by his side. "When a person has a dream and a powerful drive, it is hard to stop them," his uncle, Sean Patrick, had counseled him. Sean Patrick had stayed by his side and received his late night calls with compassion and love.

○○○

He wandered around in a fog. Through the fog, every so often, he would catch a glimpse of his precious daughter. And though it pleased him to see her getting on with life, she seemed out of reach to him. Perhaps this was because he was afraid of raising her all by himself. What did he know about raising a little girl? About haircuts and clothes and crushes on boys? He didn't know anything about female matters, about a woman's hopes and dreams. He prayed for wisdom. He prayed for strength.

He did meet other women. It seemed the easiest thing in the world not to get involved with any of them, though. He knew what they wanted. A home, a dishwasher, a car, a new Easter hat and coat, and a man on their arm. But when they had all that, they would most probably just leave him in the end, just as Nellie had. "You will never be the life of any party," Nellie had said the week before she left. "I will always love you because you are good and kind and reliable. But I can't wake up next to you another morning. You and your collection of rocks just take the umph out of my life."

How many lives, he laughed to himself, would he have to live through before he found true love? What a foolish notion, he thought and chuckled again. He was at his lab examining a curious blue piece of quartz he had found on a trek into the mountains with Kate the day before. It was shaped like no other he had seen before. Where had it come from? It was not something usually found in his area. As he continued to examine it, his thoughts wandered on. He knew that many ancient religions believed in the idea of reincarnation, how souls wandered through multiple lives until they found their way. But he was a Roman Catholic. He had a strong and solid faith. He believed in the Father, the Son and the Holy Ghost. He believed in Heaven. He believed in Hell. He was an ordinary person. He was a scientist. A simple lover of rocks. He was a lover of rain and forests and the ocean. He was a lover of nature. Just as his daughter was. He and Kate loved climbing up into the mountains together, and walking along the beach looking for stones. Especially on rainy days when there was no thunder. Sometimes they walked in the rain for hours, not even talking. Both found joy and peace of mind when the rain fell down and around them. "Climb mountains and hills. Stand in the rain. Nature washes your spirit clean," Kate had carefully written on a rock and given him to use as a paperweight at his office when she was only eight. It was his most prized possession. His dear Kate loved him. She loved him for what he was, and always would.

Between two worlds life hovers like a star.
- Lord Byron

CHAPTER TEN

THE TWO magnificent trails of turquoise and indigo blue reeled and swayed, waiting impatiently to be called. They were together, flying above the end of a night, when the next murmur, the next irresistible plea, finally came.

The turquoise flame was the first to disappear. Not long after, however, the blaze of indigo blue dove eagerly through the great divide, too.

∞

Two years after her first baby was born and given up for adoption, Poppy gave birth to a second little girl, Beatrice, who also, strangely enough, had the shape of a crescent moon above her heart. So it did not come as a surprise to her when, three years later, she gave life to a son, Peter, who also had the same birthmark of the crescent moon. "Does this run on your side of the family?" Ari asked her. "Not that I know of," she answered.

They were now living in a little Dutch farmhouse in the Hudson Valley, surrounded by woods and an acre of lovely, flat land that Poppy and Ari grew vegetables and flowers on. Poppy's painting of the small church with a single steeple hung on the wall next to their bed in the new house. She still hoped that someday, when the time was right, she might understand why she was so drawn to this place—this place in a picture that probably did not even exist.

Poppy and Ari had been in touch with the hospital where she gave birth, begging them for any and all information about Luna. But their rules were strict and unbendable. Closed adoptions were closed for a reason. Poppy was so desperate she even went to Father Sean Patrick. She pleaded with him to intervene on her behalf, and to use whatever influence he possessed to sway them. He told her that his hands were tied, too.

ooo

It was through the two children she had the privilege of keeping and loving and raising that she attempted to redeem herself. She could not allow her pain from losing her first child to take her away from them, to render her sick and unable to be the best mother she could be. All of the attention she'd previously focused on controlling everything around her and ridding herself of possessions, she now showered on them. And in this way she was able to become the person she was meant to be.

Poppy had a family and this was the most important thing to her. But she had the satisfaction of her work, too. By the time both of her children were in elementary school, she had completed her book, *The Girl On the Moon*, the first in what would become the *Luna* series. Every few years, on April 19th—the month and day she had chosen to release each of her books—children of all ages would line up at stores all over the world to purchase the next book in the series. Because she had chosen to publish under the name P.R. Doumas and did no personal publicity, her life had remained relatively unchanged, and she and Ari were able to keep their privacy, and give their children normal childhoods.

∘∘∘

LUNA AND THE CHOSEN

Luna heard its humming noise even before it came into view. It was a high-pitched, whirring kind of a sound. Instantly, her heart hurtled itself against her chest and her body began to quiver in fear. She acted without delay. Moving deliberately, imagining herself to be a particle of dust just blowing in the wind, she floated toward her nest, a few feet away, situated inside a crater. Within a blink of an eye she lowered herself into it and completely vanished.

It had been many moon-years since she had ascended. She was different now. Her body was long and strong and she was able to race for hours, never getting tired. She could jump from extremely high places and land safely by curling up and rolling like a ball that had been pitched by a streak of lightning. She had teeth that were sharp and excellent at pulling things apart. Her hair was long, so she could enfold herself in it. She could dance wildly to songs she sang at the top of her lungs, which echoed and boomed through deep craters all around.

Luna felt the shuddering of the moon's crust when the object in the sky landed. Although she was deeply concealed in her nest, everything around her quivered. Suddenly, she heard, not the dreaded thuds she had expected, but the exultant laughter of children.

Their voices rang out like bells, like chimes, tinkling and peeling at many different pitches. She had never heard sounds like it, clusters of happiness and gaiety, and it caused her to let out her breath, which she had been holding. Slowly, she allowed herself to uncurl and stir, trying to hear the chattering more clearly. And then she saw a head, then two, then three of them. Within seconds, there were many more, upside down, staring at her in wonder.

"We found you," one head called out, and giggled.

"Hide-and-seek," another announced. "How do you do? I am Wolfgang Amadeus Mozart Two."

The three children beside him introduced themselves as Joan of Arc Two, Winston Churchill Two, and Leo Tolstoy Two.

"You're very good at hiding," a small voice whispered. She was named Audrey Hepburn Two.

"Hello," another said. "I am Florence Nightingale Two. Come out, won't you, and meet us all."

As Luna climbed out of her nest, the children formed a circle around her, all holding hands. There were at least twenty of them, possibly more. She found herself dizzy with excitement and quite overwhelmed.

"Where have you all come from?" Luna begged them to tell her as she ecstatically began turning in the center of the circle so she could observe each of their faces.

"From there." The boy called Muhammad Ali Two pointed to a magnificent spacecraft, silvery and narrow, but so tall that she could barely observe the top.

"It is our home," Charlotte Brontë Two proudly told Luna.

"We were all programmed to hatch there," said a round-faced boy with a sly smile, who was named John Lennon Two.

"It's our place of origin," said a boy with sparkling eyes. "My name is Galileo Galilei Two," he said, bowing.

Her mind was working double-time struggling to identify if all they were saying was true. They may only have been children, but Luna knew by then that dangers could lurk behind even the most innocent of façades. "I am honored that you are all here and I welcome you warmly," she said, concealing her concern with a vivacious smile, but readying herself for an escape if need be.

"We are clones," Alexander Hamilton Two explained, picking up instantly on Luna's hesitation.

"Exact duplicates of important human minds who once lived on Earth," Rosa Parks Two added.

"A scientist by the name of Professor Ronald Prince was fearful that the planet Earth would destroy itself, so, in anticipation of that, he built our spacecraft with a laboratory aboard," Marie Curie Two began to explain.

"We have all the memories of our Originals, just in brand new bodies," Charles Darwin Two continued.

"The professor also assembled many kinds of robots. Robot engineers, robot educators, and robot parents, just to name a few," Golda Meir Two told Luna.

"They take care of us as we travel the Universe and wait to see what happens on Earth," William Shakespeare Two proclaimed.

"In the interim, there is so much still left to learn," Jonas Salk Two continued. "So much to try to make sense of in the world."

"We share all that we know with each other, and while the knowledge is endless, so is our capacity for learning," Mahatma Gandhi Two continued, as a diminutive boy with wild hair known as Albert Einstein Two looked on shyly.

"The robots tell us the professor was concerned about only one thing: that we wouldn't be able to get along. But we're all friends and we live in peace. This means the experiment was a success, they say," Abraham Lincoln Two said.

"So we circle in space, landing here, stopping there, and some day, if Earth does destroy itself, we will land when it is safe, and repopulate it," Maria Callas Two added.

"Well, I am so glad you have landed here," Luna told them with a sigh of relief. She was impressed with their story. Awestruck, in fact. Gradually, as she had listened to their tale, she had felt her suspicions and concerns melt away. "So, what do you want to do here?" she inquired.

"What we want is to have a party," a thin boy by the name of Socrates Two cried out excitedly.

"Yes, a birthday party. None of us has ever had a birthday party before," another boy, named Neil Armstrong Two, announced with a wide grin. "It was my idea that we come to the moon to celebrate."

"I've never had a birthday party either," Luna said excitedly.

Within seconds, the party began, as robots in bright-colored costumes over their silvery metallic bodies glided off the spacecraft. They set up decorations, tables and chairs, and giant games, and they played music. All the children sang and danced, even Luna. They played pin the tail on the donkey, had three-legged races, and broke open a gigantic piñata. There were some things called pizza and ice cream and cake. There were candles to be blown out by everyone and many wishes made. Luna had never seen anything like it before in her life. It was her very first birthday party, and she enjoyed in immensely.

As the robots cleaned up and carried everything back into the spacecraft, the children stretched out on fluffy comforters laid out for them on the ground. Luna was invited to join Georgia O'Keeffe Two and Igor Stravinsky Two.

"Will you be leaving soon?" she asked, as Georgia stroked her hand.

"Yes," Igor told her, as he leaned over to touch a lock of her golden hair. "We like it here. We especially like you. But we never stay anywhere for too long."

Luna listened to him as she lay there between them, enjoying very much the feeling of being touched. She wished she could be around them forever. With them, she felt so safe and secure. As though Georgia were reading her mind, she sat up suddenly and said, "Why don't you join us when we depart?"

"Of course, Luna, you must." Igor sat up, too, drawing Luna up with him. "A person's fears are lighter when they are shared."

When it was voted upon by all the children that Luna should accompany them, her heart danced with ecstasy and joy. She would miss the moon, of course. It had been her home for a long time now. She would especially long for her nest when she was gone. It was so snug and had shielded her from so much. Yet the thought of being surrounded with love and companionship was an even stronger pull, and she agreed to go with them. But just as she was about to step onto the spacecraft, a line of robot parents stood in her path.

"We are sorry," they told her in flat, toneless voices, which came out in clipped bursts. "We know the children want you to join them. But we have been programmed to allow only the Chosen to come aboard."

Luna stared up at them wordlessly.

They gazed back down at her with vacant eyes.

When the door of the space vessel closed, she could see faces looking out from each of the windows. There were tears in all of their eyes.

o o o

The only three people who understood why it was that Poppy decided to create the *Luna* series, and why she was compelled to keep the series going, were Ari, who was by then head of the company that published the books, and their children, Beatrice and Peter.

"Your mother and I had a baby, a little girl, before we were married," Ari explained to them when Beatrice was eleven and Peter was eight. "But we had to give her up for adoption because we were not married then, and we wanted her to have a loving mother and father and a good home." For a while there was a great quiet in the room. The clock ticked. Their old dog groaned.

It was Beatrice who spoke first. "Did you see her after she was born?" she asked, her long thin hands pressed together as in prayer.

"What did she look like? Did she look like us?" Peter wanted to know, his scruffy blond hair falling across his earnest eyes.

Ari put an arm around each child. "Are you asking if the baby had a crescent moon like you two do?" Wide-eyed, both children nodded.

"She did," Poppy answered, her eyes filling with tears. And reaching over, she gently kissed the moon mark over each of their hearts.

"I hope she'll read the *Luna* books someday," Poppy explained, "and understand that I thought of her all the time." Tears fell down her face, and Beatrice and Peter both gathered around her and held her close.

"Well, *we're* here, mommy," they assured her. "Don't worry, we'll find her one day. Or maybe she will find us."

She was the best mother she could be to her children. She found so much pleasure in them, such unbearable joy in everything they did. Yet she would continue to yearn for her firstborn. Time would never heal that continuous hurt in her soul.

°°°

On Beatrice's sixteenth birthday, Poppy took her to Paris during her spring vacation. They wandered the streets, visited Monet's Garden in Giverny, and toured the Louvre. On Easter Sunday, Poppy woke up excited to attend ten o'clock mass at Notre Dame.

"Oh, can't we sleep in this morning and go later?" Beatrice complained, when her mother opened the windows, and the rain and wind rushed in.

"We have so much to do today, darling," she sang out. "We're in Paris, ma chérie. Let's enjoy the whole day."

The teacher who is indeed wise
does not bid you to enter
the house of his wisdom,
but rather leads you to the threshold
of your mind.
- Khalil Gibran

CHAPTER ELEVEN

NOT WANTING to return home from Europe without a decision, but on the verge of running out of her savings, Kate called her father. As she knew it would, his voice immediately calmed her. She talked about all she'd done on her trip and how disappointed and afraid she was that she'd never be able to decide between marrying Scott or entering the convent. Franklyn listened quietly.

"Sweetheart, your journey isn't over yet. That's all," he finally said. "Why don't you stop in Paris on your way back home? You've always wanted to see it. This might be a good time." Then he laughed. Time had passed. Time had healed his heart. "And while you are in Paris," he said with a smirk, "look for your mother. You just might find her in the place of her dreams."

So she stopped in Paris for a day. It was a cold and rainy Easter Sunday. The youth hostel she found herself in was swarming with noisy young people, who seemed to have no idea what a bar of soap was, much less deodorant. Waking up early, she showered, packed her bag, and went off with her umbrella to get a coffee and croissant before going to Notre Dame for mass. Her father would be at Orlando Airport when she arrived that night, anxious to see her after all this time. Scott would be there too, also eager. Dear Scott. Precious Scott. Would she be breaking his heart? She took her last sip of coffee and stood at the door of the café, looking out at the pouring rain.

The cathedral was crowded when she got there. Almost every seat was taken, and it was a miracle she found one at all. Setting her bag on the floor under her legs, she leaned down, put her head in her hands and began to pray. *This is it, Bernadette. The end of the line. I have to make my choice. It's now or never. What am I going to do?*

It wasn't until the middle of mass that Kate looked up and noticed them: a mother and daughter sitting in the row in front of her. Though she could only see their backs, she felt an instant, unnerving connection to them. The girl's mother was patient, affectionate, tender, laying her arm across her daughter's shoulders, leaning over occasionally to whisper to her, smiling softly at what the girl whispered back. Kate had the urge to join them— have the mother lean over and whisper to *her*. In moments like this she missed her own mother so much, and thought how wonderful it would be to be sitting beside her now, in this beautiful place. What would her mother advise her to do? Become a nun or marry Scott? Her mother would know the answer. She would tell her, *do what makes you happiest.*

When the priest pronounced, "Let us offer one another

the sign of peace," and the congregation of thousands stirred around in their pews to join hands, Kate found herself extending her hand toward the mother, who had just turned in her direction. "Peace be with you," the mother told her in French, but with an American accent, which surprised her. The woman's hand was soft, gentle and warm. Kate wanted this moment to last forever. But then, suddenly, her hand was gone.

The mother and daughter disappeared into the crowds. Kate stood, picked up her bag, left her pew, genuflected and blessed herself and, as if in a dream, she walked towards the grand doors of the cathedral.

As she stepped out into the rain, allowing her eyes to adjust from the dark to the light, she felt her mother's voice inside her, and she smiled. "Do what makes you happiest," she heard. Letting the rain pour down around her, bathing her face, her hands, her being, she wandered through the city. She felt the wind blow against her, rearrange her hair, causing the knot on her head to become loose and fall free. She let the gusts whirl her around, and gradually, by degrees, little by little, she allowed herself to imagine what pure happiness would look like. She pictured a life with God in it, but also Scott. And she imagined motherhood. And she realized what joy all three would give her. When she finally stopped spinning, the world seemed somehow simpler—a completely new place.

The question she had been meditating on for months and months, the question that had been plaguing her for so long, the question that had been haunting her days and nights, was now not a question, after all. There was no conflict, no struggle, no decision to be made. She didn't have to be a nun to love God. She did not have to choose between Him and the man she adored. For, in fact, she could love them both. And *that* would make her happiest.

She looked around the square, seeing figures moving in the rain. Dozens of women. All with destinations that belonged to their dozens of separate lives. Any of them could be her mother, and yet somehow she knew that none of them were. She understood, then, that her mother's path and her own had diverged a long time ago. She looked deep inside her heart and found that she had accepted that her mother had a destiny separate from her own. And she knew that she would not search for her. She hoped that her mother was doing what made her happiest.

Despite the fact that she was dripping wet, her shoes soggy, and her hair stuck to the sides of her face, a long-sought peace began to rise and take her over. As she kept walking the streets, she felt such pleasure within her, she thought she might burst wide open like a fistful of flower buds just come to life.

Suddenly, she came across an old man selling wares on the street. Among the knick-knacks on display, Kate's eye caught a lovely, small canvas; the colors in it were brilliant and it made her smile. It depicted winding cobblestone streets, surrounding a small church with a single steeple.

"Où est-ce?" she asked. "Je ne sais pas," the man answered, shrugging his hunched shoulders. Despite the fact that the man could not give any details about the picture, Kate purchased it at once. This, this beautiful blustery and rainy day, she decided, felt like the first day of a new life.

°°°

On a sunny day in January, almost two years after returning from Paris, Kate Doyle gave herself to Scott and became Mrs. Kate Kennedy. She threw her bouquet of posies high into the air, and Mary Ellen, her Maid of Honor, leapt up to catch it.

Her first child, Gwen, followed soon after. Her second, Alice, joined the family a few years after that. They went to church as a family every Sunday and joined in all the church activities. Both children attended St. Anne's, the same school she had gone to. Sister Teresa was the headmistress now, and she and Kate had tea together at least twice a month, and prayed. They also talked about who Kate wanted to be outside of a wife and mother. Inspired by these conversations and her daily prayers to God, she decided to attend an Art and Design school.

"You're so talented," one of her teachers told her, pulling her aside one day while she was sketching her own design for a dress shoe. He told her of a friend who was looking for someone to help design purses. Was Kate interested? Kate was indeed interested. Within a few years, she was one of the most successful designers working at the small company. One day, she came up with an idea so charming that the elderly gentleman who had hired her and was now a friend, offered to back her.

"It's time you had your own label," he said. Kate was astonished. *Her own label*. She knew exactly what it would be.

Kate attended mass daily and felt the love of God within her; and she was happy with her days. Her children were bright, gorgeous and generous. Scott was caring and kind. And she loved her work. A day did not pass without her thanking her lucky stars.

And what of the painting she'd purchased in Paris? Kate hung it on the wall next to her side of the bed, and dreamed of someday visiting that unknown place, for which she quietly yearned.

Clouds come floating into my life,
no longer to carry rain or usher storm,
but to add color to my sunset sky.
- Rabindranath Tagore

CHAPTER TWELVE

LUNA WRAPS UP HER FOE

Luna closed her eyes, and when she opened them, she was whatever she imagined. Butterflies, she had decided, were her favorite thing. Closing her eyes, she'd imagined what it would be like, if indeed she were one. She imagined herself soaring around with multi-colored, diaphanous wings that would take her anywhere she wanted. When she opened her eyes, she was wet. She was soft. Soon, she began to feel something folded against her new body. They were wings, she discovered. The tops of her wings were blue, and the bottoms were red and brown with orange spots. At first, she could not use them the way she knew that they should be used. She needed a lot of practice. But it didn't take long for her to learn. And then, she was flying.

This new capacity of hers, she had learned the hard way, was not without risk. She had learned that she had to shut her eyes tight, not let even the slightest bit of light in, or the force that was responsible for facilitating the change, would not be vigorous enough. In fact, the first time she did it, when the idea had struck her as she lay on her golden blanket, her legs and arms spread out, she'd irksomely found herself not one thing or the other, but only a half of something. A half of a red ball that did not bounce. A gnarled, little tree with no branches. But she took her time untangling the hiccups, learning much along the way. When she had finally mastered this extraordinary gift of hers, of becoming whatever she imagined, she was relieved to discover that whatever form she changed into, she would always return to her original state within an hour or two.

After butterflies, Luna's favorite creatures were spiders. Spiders were the most accomplished of all living things, she thought. For spiders could spin webs. And spiders on the moon could spin gigantic, silky, geometrical, complex webs made of sticky, invisible threads that were as strong as steel. They could capture something as large as a horse or even an elephant.

When a moon spider catches prey, it approaches its trapped victim and uses its gigantic fangs to inject venom. This venom is extremely fast-moving and slays the prey within moments. Luna had experienced herself what it was to be apprehended and bagged in silk. But her golden curls had saved her at the very last minute, just before the fangs could insert themselves into her throat. For the sun had shone on them, making them sparkle with such intensity they appeared to be throwing off sparks of fire. Fearful, the moon spider had backed off, its giant, dark head and long, slim legs bent in a low curtsy as it went. There was a strange reverence in each of its eight shining eyes. At first, this confused Luna, as she was certain she had been close to death seconds before. But she soon understood that the glimmer in its multiple eyes signified it was fearful of her. She was the powerful one, it seemed. Because of this, it now held her in high regard, as if she were a princess, or even a queen. A princess. Luna remembered the girl with the braid, her army, and the army of Reversals. She had been a princess to them as well. *Is that who I am, then? How will I ever know for sure?* Slowly, the spider backed away in silence, joining the hundreds of others awaiting him on the horizon.

***

When they slithered toward her with their lizard-like bodies, harrowing faces, and living snakes in place of hair, an arrow of fear shot through Luna's heart. She was alone, unarmed, and not too much taller than an average Earthling of twelve. Not only were they horrendous creatures, whose hissing shrieks were spine-chilling, but they had a circle of fog around them which made them difficult to see. With her army of spiders nowhere in sight, she shut her eyes tightly and willed herself to transform into one. Lying in wait for each beast to attack, she situated herself on the tip of the web she spun extra firm, five times the strength of steel. Then, as each monster approached, she spun it quick as lightening into a round, bulky, plump sack, enclosing it completely. But the more she captured, the more they multiplied. Alarmed, she saw that her spider web was filling up and was on the verge of tearing apart.

Then, suddenly, her time as a spider came to an end, and she was standing before them, once again, in the body of a girl.

ooo

The first feature film adapted from P.R. Doumas's *Luna* series arrived in theaters around the world on April 19, 2000. Ari's company now had to get millions of newly-printed special editions of the first book out to thousands of booksellers, who were responsible for getting them into the hands of millions of screaming and fainting fans. Poppy had nothing to do that particular day, as she was avoiding everything and everyone. She was grateful that Ari was taking care of it all. In fact, she was wearing a wide-brimmed hat and sunglasses, and wandering a street in Paris on the Left Bank, thinking about April 19th and why the date was so important to her. Her firstborn would be thirty-five years old today.

It was then that she saw it in the window of Le Bon Marché, a department store on the corner of Rue du Bac and Rue de Sèvres. She approached and, her hands pressed to the glass, she leaned in as close as she could. It was only a purse. But written on the inside of the open flap were words that struck her with an extraordinary force. And then she saw the label, with an image that looked just like her picture of the church with the single steeple. She went inside and found a sales clerk.

"May I see the purse in the window?" she asked her.

"Oh, but Madame. It is so difficult to climb in. It is high up and *dangereux*. We have other purses by the same designer. Please come. They are over here."

Poppy shook her head. "I am sorry to trouble you. But it is the one in the window that I want. No other."

"I understand, Madame," the sales lady nodded. As she labored to climb up into the display window, she chatted away.

"The designer makes each one different. There are no two alike. Let me explain. It's the quote inside, you see? Each purse has a unique one, meant just for the woman who carries it."

She handed the purse to Poppy, who nearly seized it out of the woman's hand. The first touch of the leather made her heart melt. It really did feel like the purse had been crafted especially for her. The quote was handwritten in gold, cursive letters. *Three things cannot be long hidden*, it said, *the sun, the moon, and the truth*.

ooo

Dear Ms. Kennedy, she wrote that night.

I am in Paris and have just purchased one of your purses. It is absolutely beautiful, and one of my most prized possessions. I feel that the quote inside was written just for me.

I have a question for you. The picture of the small church on your label interests me very much. Can you tell me about it? Where you found it, where this neighborhood is... any information you may have will be greatly appreciated.

Many Thanks,
Poppy Russell Doumas

Death is no more than passing
from one room into another.
- Helen Keller

CHAPTER THIRTEEN

KATE stared at the tray of mail that had come in that morning. She was exhausted. She had been in meetings all day, discussing the inclusion of her purses in shows at the upcoming Milan Fashion Week. All she wanted now was to go home, take off her shoes, and make a delicious dinner for Scott, her daughters, Alice and Gwen, and her father. The mail was shoved aside.

Her father had been living with them for a while. The Kennedy house was more than large enough to accommodate the five of them. When his grandchildren were younger, and Kate and Scott were busy with work, Franklyn Doyle was the one to take them to school in the mornings and pick them up in the afternoons. He was a soft-spoken man with a constant twinkle in his eye, and he was beloved by all because of the calm he brought to the highly kinetic household.

Scott, a photographer who sold his work to a variety of magazines, was out before the crack of dawn, shooting pictures of surfers, seascapes, and the stunning Florida shoreline. Kate's business was expanding daily. She found herself having to travel a lot, not only to cities around America but all around Europe, as well. She hated leaving her family. It tore her apart at times. Knowing this, Franklyn had taken to sneaking little notes into the side pocket of her suitcase, to read when she got to her destination. Each time she opened his envelopes her heart would swell with joy. It was Franklyn, more often than not, who packed Alice and Gwen's lunches, made breakfast and took care of household chores. The fact that Kate's family all lived together in one big, bright, beautiful house on the beach, was ideal. And life was ideal for ten years, in which the girls grew and flourished. Ideal, that is, until Franklyn was diagnosed with terminal cancer. After that, everything changed.

°°°

Kate could see the distance growing in her father's usually-bright eyes. "You are the best dad I could ever have had," she told him late one afternoon, as she stroked his cheek. "I hope you know how much I love you."

Franklyn's death was not a peaceful one. It was not graceful as the man himself had been in life. It was anything but graceful. When the end came, he began to choke. His entire body shook. He fought with all he had left in him against the inevitable. "I've got you, Dad. I've got you," she whispered, as she held him close. And, in her arms, he took his last breath, and was gone.

∞

He was no longer weak. He was no longer fragile. His breath was effortless. All limitations were gone.

He began to hum. It was a sweet hum. It was the sound of a dream come true.

∞

After Franklyn's body was taken away by the paramedics, Scott begged Kate to take a walk with him on the beach. Completely numb and nestled under his arm, Kate put one foot in front of the other, grateful for the consistent crashing of the waves and the calls of the seagulls overhead.

When she heard the humming, she looked up. "What is that?" she asked Scott, looking around. "Where is it coming from?" she wondered aloud. "It's so beautiful..."

∘∘∘

Kate closed down her warehouse and office for a month. She needed to be alone with Scott, Alice, and Gwen. The house was so silent without her father's laughter, his silly songs from the forties, his puttering around. Her grieving was deep and intense.

"What are we going to do without Grandpa?" Alice sobbed on Kate's shoulder.

"I miss him so much," Gwen whispered.

∞

He felt wide-open, clean and clear. The edges of him, his shadow, fused and dissolved into the expanse. He was infinite now. Eternal. He was outside of time.

∞

"Franklyn was a good man, Kate. One in a million," Scott said, looking at a photo album.

"I'm glad I was with him at the end," she replied, wrapped in a quilt, her head resting on Scott's shoulder.

She couldn't stop shivering. It seemed she was cold all the time now.

∞

"Where am I?" he asked.

"You're here. You're back," they told him.

"We are born knowing everything," they explained. "But with each passing day we recall a little less."

"Nothing is forever," they whispered. "We come, we go, and then we are back again."

"Each time we are just a little bit changed. We are like a blaze that boils water in an old copper pot, and becomes a spray of mist, absorbed by the parched lips of a man in need of hope."

∞

Kate stood looking out the kitchen window. She missed her father so much. Her heart had ached continuously since his passing. The palms of her hands moved along the uneven wood chopping board he had made for her a few years before. Everything around reminded her of him. The rock garden he had built for her that now overflowed with herbs. The watercolor he had painted that hung over the living room fireplace. The stack of white envelopes with her name scribbled across the fronts, containing his notes, and kept in her bedside table drawer. She could no longer catch the scent of the sweet cologne he wore, though. For at least two weeks she had smelled hints of it when she wandered around the house. Now, all she could smell was the weather changing.

The news report had warned of a storm. It would be the

first of the season. Scott and the girls had gone out and were due back any minute. She was chopping vegetables for a soup, and all she could think of, as the tears ran down her face, was that her father had departed and there was no hope of ever seeing him again.

∞

A drop of rain clinging to a window, he looked in and saw a solitary form, mourning. He desperately wanted to go to her, ease her pain, take it away.

"We are, none of us, ever alone," they murmured as they coasted around him. "We are forever a part of all things."

∞

Kate scooped up the chopped vegetables. She let them fall into the broth, now boiling on the stove. Drops of rain were gliding down the kitchen window. In the distance, she saw a bolt of lightning and, some seconds later, heard the crash of thunder. The wind was picking up, and she could see the trees begin to tilt outside. The Australian pine that her father had planted with Gwen when she was three was waving and tipping in the wind. She began to worry about it and about Scott and the girls.

And then suddenly, everything stopped. Everything was still.

"That was quite a storm," Alice said when she arrived home with Gwen and Scott.

"Did you see that rainbow?" Scott asked.

"It's Grandpa," Gwen said with a grin wide across her face. "He just wanted to say hello."

"You're right," Kate said, giving them all hugs.

Somewhere, something incredible
is waiting to be known.
- Carl Sagan

CHAPTER FOURTEEN

POPPY carried her handbag with the quote in it everywhere. When she got home at night she put it on the stool next to the kitchen counter and throughout the evening and in the morning, she would glance over at it, and a small smile would appear on her face. When things went wrong, like when a shipment of personally-signed Spanish editions of the *Luna* books went astray on their way to an orphanage in Colombia; or one of her children was having a problem; or her computer crashed and she hadn't saved what she had written that day, she would automatically, without even thinking about it, reach for her bag, hold it close to her, smell the reassuring scent of its leather and, like a drug, it would calm her almost immediately. It was irrational, she knew, but she didn't care.

Her father and Uncle Fitz were long dead, and her mother and Jane were old now. Though they seldom visited, they did write to one another and spoke on the phone occasionally. Her parents and Jane had been a peripheral part of her life since reconnecting years after she'd left home. After Beatrice and Peter were born, and became old enough to ask about their grandparents, Poppy hadn't had the heart to keep them completely apart, though she did keep them at arm's length. She always feared that if they got too close, they would interfere with her family, and she didn't want to take that chance ever again. They had accepted Ari as her children's father. They were extremely proud of Poppy's success as a writer, and kept dozens of copies of her books to hand out to everyone they knew.

Beatrice and Peter, who now had families of their own, had loved her parents and her aunt and uncle. They had some of their grandparents' characteristics, which she'd always wondered about, since they'd seen one another only once a year, for a week in the summers. Beatrice, for example, had a way of writing notes to herself to remind her of everything, just like her mother had done. When Poppy was growing up, she found notes like: *Clean silver in living room, Go to Molino's for shanks of lamb*, and *Order flowers for dinner party*, pasted to the icebox. On Beatrice's bedroom wall the same kind of scribbled little notes appeared all through her adolescence. *Party at Agatha's bring chips, thank you letter to Granny & Grandpa* and *ear piercing with Kami*. Peter, like his grandfather, had a great love of reading. Her father would send him very valuable first edition antiquarian leather-bound books from his own shelves.

There was a stone-cold place in her heart, however, that just wouldn't let her forgive her mother *completely*. While she no longer had the same depth of rage that she carried in her youth, she would never get over the feeling of being deeply harmed by her. "You have nothing to offer this baby," she remembered her mother hissing into her ear. "Nothing at all. And to think that you do, is greedy, reckless, and irresponsible." A day did not pass that she didn't remember those words. And a day did not pass that she did not think about Luna, where she was, what she was doing, and whether she'd ever see her again. Right from the start, the *Luna* series had been a way for Poppy to remain connected to her firstborn as she grew up. The character in her books and her long lost daughter were one and the same, after all.

LUNA AND THE SHADOW

It was time for Luna to move. The thought of it devastated her, for she loved her cozy little nest, and it had been her home for so many years. But in the last weeks the nest had become smaller and almost impossible for her to climb down into it, or, up out of. It had become so uncomfortable, in fact, that she could no longer stretch out when she slept. *There is no getting around it*, she'd thought to herself.

If anything, Luna was a pragmatic sort of person; sensible and levelheaded. She began to collect her belongings and thrust them up through the nest's opening, to move to the new crater she'd found. *I am brave and courageous and fearless*, she informed herself heartily, with only a speck of self-doubt. *I am brave and courageous and fearless*, she repeated, only this time louder, fiercer, and very authoritatively. Her possessions, however, seemed to be stuck, and no matter how much she pushed, they remained immovable, halfway up and halfway down.

I am also the solver of problems, she reminded herself. *I have patience, fortitude, determination*, she bellowed as she pushed some more. *Patience, fortitude, determination*, she roared again for good measure, as saying things twice gave her more power. And then, with a sudden pop, she heard her possessions break through. No longer blocked, the light from above shone down on her and she lay back.

That's when Luna saw what had been blocking the entrance. It was a box wrapped with a pink ribbon. Inside was a note, and under it was something wrapped in white gossamer wings. Holding her breath, she carefully removed layers of feathers until she found what they were protecting. It was so light that she could barely feel it. Grayish-black in color, it was folded into a perfect square. *What is this*, she wondered, as she unfolded the note.

Dearest Luna,

This is a shadow. Put it on and it will transport you to one mind. One mind only. Of any person you choose. Only one person, remember. So choose carefully. To return to your body on the moon, take off the shadow. It will evaporate. It can't be used again.

Fondly Your Friend,

Albert Einstein Two

Luna didn't need to deliberate long. She knew immediately whom she would select, for she had thought of this person every moment of her life on the moon. Unfolding the shadow gingerly, as it was sticky, she cautiously spread it over herself.

In a flash, without any warning, she was there. Plunked right in the center of her mother's mind.

And her mother's mind was crowded... with thoughts only of her.

We shall find peace. We shall be angels;
we shall see the sky sparkling with diamonds.
- Anton Chekhov

CHAPTER FIFTEEN

THE YEAR was 1892. Even before the sun revealed the tiniest sliver of first light, Bakha was standing with his twig broom and basket, waiting in silence as though he were not there. He loved witnessing the beginning of day when the dark evaporates and dissolves into gray. It thrilled his heart each morning, seeing hundreds of ghostlike figures wrapped in white, wordlessly rise from where they had been sleeping on the street around him, and drift like silvery spirits to the fountain. It exhilarated him to hear the splashing water when they washed themselves in the fabric they wore, letting it dry as they moved on to start the day.

Bakha was an Untouchable, a boy from the lowest class in India. But he was an outcast even among the Untouchables for the highly unusual misfortune of having been born with red hair. He was abandoned by his family and ostracized by everyone else who lived on the streets because, to them, red hair was the mark of a curse. He had been an orphan for as long as he could remember. And for almost as long, he had been coating his hair with mud, dulling it to a stiff, bleak brown.

As the sun rose and warmed his little body, Bakha bent over his broom, and began systematically sweeping the gutter in front of him, clearing it of human waste. He knew not to abandon his focus, no matter how hungry he was, no matter how thirsty he became. He knew not to make eye contact as he worked. He knew not to frown or smile. He knew never to look back if there was a commotion or look up when a stranger addressed him. Most importantly, he knew not to touch or be touched by anyone. Not ever.

Bakha could neither read nor write, but he had been blessed with the ability to recall everything he ever heard. The stories spoken by strangers as they passed by, the friendly greetings exchanged by the merchants in their booths each morning, the verses recited by children in singsong voices came to his ears, and all of these were carefully recorded in Bakha's mind. He remembered every detail. And as his body worked diligently, his mind was able to wander into all of the lives and diverse experiences he would never be able to have himself. He never stopped sweeping. Not until the day ended and the gray slid seamlessly into black again.

But that afternoon, everything would change. She came out of nowhere, it seemed. A white woman in a straw hat and embroidered skirts knelt down in front of him and grinned. In her outstretched palm was an offering of food. "For you," she said softly. "It's cake." Suddenly, his rhythm was broken. He stumbled back. Although he understood nothing she said, it was clear to him that she was offering the food. He heard his stomach growl. This noise, which sounded like thunder to him, caused a great heat of shame to cover his small, round face. "Go on," the white woman insisted, moving the cake closer to him. It was like something out of his imagination. This couldn't be real. Bakha reached out hesitantly and took the cake. And a fear unlike anything he'd known gripped him, because he realized that for a brief second he'd touched, ever so slightly, her soft hand. In that very moment, as the horror of what had happened threatened to topple him, an exuberant, tender part of him wanted more than anything to feel that touch again.

"Stop, you pig, you son of a dirty dog," a man shouted at him from behind. He felt a blow to his ribs, another to his back, and several to his head. As he crumbled to the ground in a heap, his fingers opened, and the cake fell out of his hand.

Confused, alarmed, then terrified, the woman with the straw hat screamed out, "Stop. Please. He is just a little boy."

The man smiled. He spoke to her in English. "Madam, you must leave right now. This filthy urchin is not what he seems. He is swine, full of diseases and germs. You may be contaminated. Go and wash yourself."

The woman's eyes filled with tears. "It is my first day here in Bombay. I saw him from the balcony up there," she said, turning to point up at the hotel nearby. "He looked so hungry and I have so much. I just thought..." The woman was unable to finish. Whirling around, she ran away.

The man turned back and continued kicking Bakha where he lay on the ground. "You have touched this woman and defiled her, you vile, useless piece of garbage!" Bakha was used to being spoken to roughly, spit on and kicked about. Soon, he thought, it would all come to an end. But a crowd had begun to gather around him, their eyes flaming. Instinctively, he joined his hands together in apology for his behavior, but the crowd didn't care.

Blood ran over his face and his vision blurred. As he closed his eyes for the last time and darkness fully enveloped him, the pain he felt blotted out every thought but one: he held tightly to the memory of the woman's kindness and how the only magic he had ever known in his short life was the touch of her hand. *In my next life,* he vowed to himself, *I will not die and disappear unnoticed. By some means,* he promised himself as he let out his final breath, *I must bring something essential into this world when I return again.*

∞

He was back, and immediately he remembered it all.

He circled the past, the present, and the yet-to-be, humming jubilantly, so happy to be home again.

∞

The first thing the woman in the hat did when she returned to the hotel was to go into her room and bolt the door. Drawing the curtains, she rendered the room as dark as she could. Her body trembled with fear.

She stripped her clothing off, and scrubbed herself over and over, using up all the water in the pitcher next to the chamber pot. When her skin was rubbed raw, she stumbled onto the bed and screwed her eyes shut, trying to silence the roar of the crowd outside.

And then she heard the hum.

∞

He was the thick veil of smoke rising from the cooking fires, seeping in through the windows, that filled each breath she took with forgiveness and tranquility. He was a skipping stone, a passing fancy. He was a sprig of parsley plucked by the fingers of a Parisian girl...

Abruptly, he was jerked away by an ear-splitting screech, a squawk, a high-pitched howl. In the blink of an eye, he found himself, with no warning at all, once again on the other side of the great, imperceptible divide.

∞

It was the early 1990s, and like everything else at the time, the baby was in a hurry to be born. She slid out on the kitchen floor before her mother had time to even lie down. "She could be a little Lucille Ball," her father said in wonder. "Look at all that curly red hair." They did end up calling her Lucille Semblance, and eventually, Lucy for short.

Lucy was an extraordinarily beautiful baby. But there was also something else about her that caught people and stopped them in their tracks. From the moment she was born, wherever her mother took her, people would stoop over her carriage and gasp. "Oh, what a tender little soul she is," they would say, shaking their heads in awe. "Just look at that pure love pouring out of her."

No one has a right to consume happiness
without producing it.
- Helen Keller

CHAPTER SIXTEEN

BY THE time Lucy Semblance was eleven months old, she could speak in sentences. By the time she was three, she could read. What she was really good at, however, was remembering things. All her parents had to do was say a sentence once, and she could repeat it back without a mistake. She knew by heart all the dialogue from every film her parents let her watch. Films were her favorite thing in the world. The characters in the movies she liked became a part of her life. She had entire conversations with them in her head, and thought of them as her friends. From the moment she knew what dreams were, she dreamt of becoming an actress herself. And she was talented. She auditioned for and was cast in several commercials at first, and soon made her way to featured roles on television. Casting directors absolutely loved Lucy because she was mature enough to take on the demands of working, but looked so small for her age; lithe and with the cheeks of a cherub, she could easily play roles years younger than herself. The directors and producers she worked with told her mother that she would go far.

One day, Lucy's agent called, her voice bubbling with excitement. "Lucy has an offer for the lead in a big movie. They need her to start shooting at the beginning of next week. The only thing is she will have to change the color of her hair. The character of Luna is blonde."

While her mother stuck Lucy's head into their kitchen sink and transformed the color of her hair from shiny red to shiny platinum blond, Lucy could hardly contain the unbelievable joy she felt. She had begun reading the *Luna* books a year ago, and that she would now *become* Luna was more than she could ever have dreamed of. She wondered if other little girls who saw her in the films would consider her *their* friend.

°°°

The next day, Lucy and her mother flew from Brooklyn to California, and were met at the airport by a black limousine, which took them straight to Warner Bros. Studios, in Burbank. They drove past the guard gate at the main entrance to the massive studio, and down an avenue lined with gigantic, boxy, windowless buildings looking like aircraft hangars, each one marked with a number.

When they were ushered out of the limousine in front of a building marked STAGE 22, Lucy was nearly run down by a man on a bike riding very fast. As her mother grabbed her hand and pulled her back, they found themselves in the path of a team of horses ridden by gladiators. Flattening themselves against the limousine, they waited until the narrow street was clear and, just as they were about to move again, were stopped by a group of rambunctious children spilling out of a classroom bungalow across the way. One of them, a girl, covered head to toe in glitter and sparkles, stepped out of the crowd, looked straight at Lucy, and smiled.

She was the exact size and build, with the same blue eyes, same nose and mouth, and same length and color of hair as Lucy. In fact, she was the mirror image of Lucy. Lucy gaped.

"Hi, I'm Evelyn," the girl said, smiling. "I'm gonna be your stand-in."

"My what?" Lucy inquired as agreeably as she could, considering the fact that she felt a sudden wariness of this girl reaching out to take her hand.

"You've never had a stand-in before?" Evelyn asked. "Well, I'll explain it all to you," she began pompously. "Whenever they're setting lights or things like that, they get me to stand in for you so you don't get too hot or tired. It's real hard being a stand-in. I am very important."

∘∘∘

Lucy's mother did not like it that Evelyn was around all the time. "What's that girl want anyway?" she asked Lucy one day. "She irritates me."

"I just feel sorry for her," Lucy said. She was sitting cross-legged on the floor of her trailer with the film script. She glanced over the open page in front of her, committed all her dialogue to memory within moments, and flipped to the next page. "She has a lot of brothers and sisters in Minnesota, and her father ran off, so everyone is dependent on her. She's kind of like the father of the family and sends them all money. That has to be hard. And she's here with just her older sister. I try to be nice to her. And she does have a boring job just sitting around while everyone else gets to do interesting things."

"Well, I'd keep an eye out for her if I were you," Lucy's mother warned.

Lucy flipped page after page, as her mother looked on, still amazed, after all these years, by her daughter's ability to retain so much information with so little effort. Suddenly, Evelyn walked through the door.

"Knock first, will you," Lucy's mother said. "You know that. I've told you before."

"I forgot. I'm sorry," Evelyn said. "I wanted to tell you that lunch has been called. So do you want to go over to Bob's Big Boy and get a hamburger and French fries, Lucy?"

"No, she doesn't," Lucy's mother answered firmly. "She wants something healthy to eat. And so should you."

○○○

"She never lets Lucy go anywhere," Evelyn said, smiling to her sister in the car as the two of them drove the few blocks to Bob's. "And that's just fine by me."

When the two sisters walked into Bob's, they were seated at the best booth right away, even though the place was crowded. "Hey there, Lucy. How are you doing today?" the waitress asked.

"Oh, I'm very good, Melba," answered Evelyn, smiling. "How are you?"

"Well, I am just as excited as can be for your movie to come out. I'm a big fan of the books, you know. I think everyone is. I know you've already given me one, but could I have another autograph, please? It's for my sister,

Mabel. She doesn't believe I know you."

Evelyn smiled up at her. "Sure I can Melba. Should I just use this napkin?"

"Oh yes," the waitress giggled. "Do you have your special pen?"

"I do," Evelyn answered, and took it out from her shiny red purse. The pen was a glittery sky blue. She reached for the napkin in front of her, and just like an old pro, she wrote: To Mabel, from your friend, Luna.

° ° °

Though Lucy had met P.R. Doumas briefly on the previous shoots, it wasn't until the third movie, being shot at Pinewood Studios in England, that she was able to spend considerable time with her at Fortnum & Mason, over afternoon tea. They were sitting out of sight from the other customers in The Drawing Room, and Lucy was enjoying having the author of the *Luna* books all to herself.

"Is it all right with you that we're so hidden away?" Poppy asked.

"Oh, of course," Lucy replied. "You're so famous. I understand."

"Well, you're famous, too." Poppy smiled as she reached over, poured the tea into their bone china cups, and offered Lucy one of the cucumber sandwiches from the three-tiered silver tray placed between them. "In fact," she continued, "you might just be more famous than me."

Not knowing what to say, Lucy took a bite of her sandwich and a sip of her tea.

"Haven't you noticed at all the opening nights, when we are walking down the red carpet, all the fans are screaming for you?"

Lucy took another sip of tea and looked down into her lap.

"Don't you like being famous?" Poppy asked.

Lucy shook her head. She felt tongue-tied.

"I don't either. But it has to be harder for you. Everywhere you go people recognize you. With me, it's different. I don't have long blond hair. And I don't wear glitter."

Lucy looked up and laughed in surprise. "Oh, that's not me who wears the glitter. That's Evelyn, my stand-in. She tells everyone that she is me and they believe her. She even signs my name on things."

Poppy's eyes widened in astonishment. "Really!" she said.

"Oh, it doesn't bother me that much. She gets such a kick out of it. She's obsessed with being rich and famous, I guess. I don't care so much about that, as long as I get to keep acting."

Poppy stared at Lucy and listened to her, very impressed, as she talked on.

"And while people may think Evelyn is me on the street, I'm the one who gets to open the letters children write to me. And there is nothing else like it. I have you to thank for this, of course. If it wasn't for you, there would be no Luna and I wouldn't be who I am."

Poppy smiled. "No, sweet girl, it's I who have you to thank. Because of you I get to see a living, breathing version of my beloved Luna out in the world. Someone who in all these years only existed in my imagination. And it gives me such joy to see how much you love playing the role."

"I really, truly do. I know this sounds silly, but since I was little, all I wanted was to be able to touch people... just like you do. And maybe I do, maybe just a little bit, because I get the loveliest letters from fans who feel they can say anything to me, who share their dreams with me."

"Your parents must be so proud of you. I know I am. Do you get to spend a lot of time with them between movies?" Poppy asked.

"My mom is with me all the time, but my dad had to move from New York to Kansas to run a manufacturing plant there. When I'm not working, we go and live with him. Do you want to know a secret?" she asked Poppy.

Poppy nodded and leaned in.

"Underneath all this blond, my real hair is red, and I mean red. I love it. When I am back home in Kansas, Mom dyes it red so I can go back to being who I really am."

"So no one recognizes you in Kansas, either?"

"Nope," Lucy shook her head. "Only my best friend, Albert Einstein Three, my dog."

That made Poppy laugh so hard she almost spilled her tea.

○○○

The *Luna* movies were so popular that when each new one opened, people began to stand in line the day

111

before. Evelyn did not like it when, by the time the fourth one came to the screen, people had begun to realize she was not Lucy when she was out in public. Although she and Lucy had looked almost identical when they were younger, they were growing up to look quite different. She was grateful to appear so young for her age, just as Lucy did, but it distressed Evelyn nonetheless that they were dissimilar enough now that she wasn't able to receive the attention she craved any longer. And she decided to do something about it.

Eight months before the fifth *Luna* movie was scheduled to shoot in Cape Town, South Africa, Evelyn went to a plastic surgeon with pictures of Lucy, and had her nose and chin reconstructed, so they looked exactly like hers.

000

Lucy and her mother loved Cape Town. They loved the beauty and the flatness of the land that stretched out before them forever, the vibrancy of life there, the mixture of cultures, the music and the art.

Evelyn hated it there. She thought the city was dirty and ugly. She didn't leave her hotel except to go to the studio. She missed her life in Hollywood and her boyfriend. She had become an emancipated minor and lived in an apartment with Roger. But Evelyn didn't want to be a stand-in anymore. What she wanted was for someone to stand in for her.

It was in Cape Town, while watching a murder mystery on TV, that Evelyn came up with the idea. And it was there in her small hotel room that she began to work out the plot of how she would take over Lucy's part in the last movie of the series, and finally become Luna herself.

ooo

A week after the shoot, Lucy came back to Los Angeles to do some pick-up dialogue. She was walking down Melrose Avenue in a baseball cap and sunglasses, going in and out of second-hand shops searching for dresses from the 1940s, when a mud-spattered black Suzuki motorcycle jumped up onto the sidewalk and hit her.

There were two riders on it, onlookers told the police later. But because they were covered from head to toe in black and wore helmets, no one could give a description. The license plate was unreadable as, like the bike, it too was covered in mud.

Badly injured, Lucy sunk into a coma. Her parents both stayed by her side, holding her hand, talking and reading to her night and day. Poppy visited often. Evelyn tried to come, but Lucy's parents had her barred from the room. "You're not family," Lucy's mother shrieked at her in the hallway, tears smearing her face.

"I'm kind of like family after all these years," Evelyn said, smiling at Roger when she arrived home. "And now I'll be more than family. I will actually *be* her. We're shooting the last movie in Europe and they're going to have to cast me as Luna for that one!"

But it never happened. A week later, Roger was arrested for running down Lucy. He had a criminal record for shoplifting from a few years earlier, and the thumbprint on the gas cover of the Suzuki the police found ditched in the desert matched the prints on record. It didn't take the police long to get him to confess. He held out a full week before telling them about Evelyn's involvement.

At her court arraignment Evelyn wore purple glitter all over her face. The press went wild. Instantly, her picture was on the internet. Newspapers around the world published her story, while photographs of her growing up on all the *Luna* sets appeared on the front pages of magazines in twenty different countries. There was even a book being written about her.

"Well, I got what I wanted," she told her cellmate. "I'm a big star now. Bigger than *she* will ever be."

∘∘∘

When Lucy finally opened her eyes, she was surrounded by the most glorious, overwhelming fragrance that enveloped all her senses. And every color imaginable blurred together in front of her eyes. She blinked several times. Breathed in slowly, calmly. Soon, everything began to fall into place, each of the colors gained focus, and became one of the hundreds and hundreds of flowers around her room. There were just as many get-well cards sent by girls and boys from all around the world. Everyone, it seemed, had been praying for Lucy to wake up.

And there were her parents, smiling down at her, their faces tear-streaked. "Welcome back," they said.

Everything you can imagine is real.

- Pablo Picasso

CHAPTER SEVENTEEN

A R I   W A S not only the publisher of all the *Luna* books but, after the first film adaptation was made, he also became the executive producer of the rest of the movies. *Luna Takes Wing*, the last in the series, was to be shot in Prague. Ari would be directing this one himself. Poppy was proud and thrilled. It had always been a dream of theirs that he direct one.

°°°

"I don't want you to be on the set for the first few days," Ari told Poppy a few weeks before the first day of shooting. They were in Prague, having tea in the lobby of the Four Seasons Hotel, overlooking the Vltava River.

"I wouldn't make a sound," Poppy said. "I never do. I'll be like a fly on the wall. I promise."

Ari reached over and took her hand.

"I won't even talk to you," she pleaded. "No clapping when the first scene ends. Nothing. You won't even know I'm there."

He brought her hand up to his mouth and kissed it.

"Oh, Ari. We always do things together. All along we've

been together on this. It's my baby."

"I know," he told her. "It's just the first few days. Until I feel secure... maybe the first two weeks."

"The first two *weeks*," Poppy said, pulling her hand back and looking him in the eyes.

"It's a new crew," he told her. "A new location. Some new cast members. And it's my first time directing, Poppy. I know what I'm doing. I have no doubts about my abilities. I've got it all storyboarded. I've got Jonathan. Since he's been the cinematographer on all of them, if I need help he'll be there. But I just can't look over and see you standing there when I say *action* for the first time."

"Why not?" she asked, tears welling in her eyes.

He reached over and tucked a strand of hair behind her ear.

"Because..." he told her, "I might get a little intimidated."

"Intimidated." Poppy laughed. "Why would I intimidate you? I'm just your wife."

Ari's thick, dark hair had begun graying on the sides. Like Poppy, he had developed laugh lines around his eyes. They had been with each other for over forty years now. They knew one another so well. They loved each other so much. And after all they had gone through together they had great respect for one another.

Poppy took a deep breath. "Jonathan has an apartment in Paris," she said. "He told me I could use it any time I wanted during this shoot. It might be fun staying in a place I've never been before."

Later that night, Ari and Poppy returned to their room on the highest floor of the hotel and stood together looking out the great windows at the ancient city, its twinkling lights reflecting in the Vltava below. Ari wrapped his arms around her and pulled her close. She could feel his heart beating hard against her chest, and they just stood there together for a while, in silence.

ooo

Poppy flew from Prague to Paris a week later, with a hat pulled down over her head, a pair of sunglasses, a carry-on suitcase, which she stuck above, and her purse, which she held on to for the two-hour trip. She didn't know why, but she was close to tears. She tried to read the magazine she had bought at the newsstand but the type just blurred together, so finally, she put it down. What was wrong with her? She loved Paris. She was excited to be staying in an apartment there. She was looking forward to wandering, exploring, finding new nooks and crannies in her favorite city. She appreciated that Ari needed to establish himself as the main force on the set without any competition from her. She was the writer, the creator. Ever since the movies had come out, it had become impossible to remain hidden. The press loved her. Everyone recognized her. She was always being surrounded and asked for her autograph. And Ari was right in the fact that she would draw attention no matter how hard she tried not to. But it was Lucy's first time back on set since coming out of her coma, and Poppy wanted to be there for her. Also, she had always been there for the first shot of all of the movies. It was her baby... and as unreasonable as it was... by being asked to leave... she felt like she was abandoning Luna... yet again. She couldn't control it. Her body began to tremble and her heart ached so hard she thought she could be having a heart attack. Covering her face, she turned towards the window to hide, letting the tears flow freely out of her.

∘∘∘

Charles de Gaulle airport was socked in with fog, and it took the plane longer than normal to land. When she exited the airport to get a taxi, it was raining so hard she could barely see anything in front of her. Once the taxi was on the road, Poppy called Ari to say she had landed, and wished him luck for the first day of filming the next day.

Despite the fact that it was almost midnight, the traffic into the city was slow. The taxi drove through the heart of Paris, and then wound up and down narrow streets, to the address that she had handed the driver. The rain was coming down in such thick sheets, she could not see the apartment building until the driver helped her out and kindly took her to the entrance door.

Jonathan had warned her about the light in the hallway going out every thirty seconds and that she would have to push the switch on every floor to get it back on again. *How charming*, she had thought. But now, on the second floor, soaking wet and exhausted, fumbling for the switch in total darkness while holding on to her dripping suitcase and purse, she wished she had gone to the Paris Ritz. On the third floor, she put the giant key Jonathan had given her into the gigantic lock, opened the door, found the single bedroom, stripped naked, threw on her nightgown, and fell onto the bed.

∘∘∘

She slept until the bright sun, shining in and around the

edges of the long red velvet drapery, burst through and woke her. Slipping out of bed, she thanked God that it had stopped raining, and went to the window, drawing back the heavy drapes. And then she gasped.

She pulled open the French doors and stepped out onto the balcony, just as the church bells began to ring. Wrapping herself in her arms, she stared out at the winding cobblestone streets below, surrounding church with a single steeple.

The energy of the mind is the essence of life.

- Aristotle

CHAPTER EIGHTEEN

TOMORROW would be Kate's first trip away from home since her father had died. She had to be up at five in the morning to catch an eight-fifteen flight to Paris, for a week of meetings. She wasn't looking forward to it. She seldom, if ever, enjoyed traveling for work. If she could have found someone else to step into her shoes, she would have done it in a heartbeat. But it was her that they all wanted to see and talk to. It was her that they wanted to throw the parties for. It was her that they wanted to toast. But, she reminded herself, she still had today. And tonight, she and Scott would be going over to Mary Ellen and Tom's for dinner. Their son, Tom, Jr., had just returned from a year abroad studying architecture. Tommy, as Kate called him, was her godson.

Mary Ellen had married Tom Bates right after college. Tom founded and led the choir at St. Anne's small parish during Kate and Mary Ellen's senior year. He had arrived with some fanfare as the new organist and choirmaster. He was soon much beloved by all for his energetic organ solos and his good looks. The moment Mary Ellen had set eyes on him, she'd told Kate she was going to faint.

"I'm going to marry that man," she'd announced. And by God, she had.

Now, decades later, Tom Bates was still the choirmaster of St. Anne's, which had doubled in size over the years, with the help of Kate and Mary Ellen's fundraising. Mary Ellen was a real estate agent. In fact, she was one of the leading real estate agents in Florida. She had worked hard day and night for years, and deserved every accolade thrown her way. Both she and Tom were also excellent cooks, and between the two of them, meals at the Bates home were relished by all.

o o o

"The main event of the evening is Tommy's return," Mary Ellen announced. She grinned at her son as she placed a laptop at the center of the dining room table when dinner was finished. "He took some amazing pictures while he was traveling around. And we are so proud of him."

"Oh, Mom," Tommy said, rolling his eyes. "Anyone could have taken these pictures. Don't make Kate and Scott sit through..."

"No, we want to see them," Scott interrupted. "After all, I did give you your first camera, Tommy. This is very exciting. I may learn a thing or two."

Kate loved Tommy and Mary Ellen and Tom, but as much as she wanted to look at all the pictures her godson had taken on his trip, she was exhausted from her busy day, knowing that tomorrow, her travel day, would be even more tiring.

She wanted to stand and give her excuses—until the

first picture appeared on the screen. When she saw it, she let out a breath and grabbed Tommy's arm.

"Where is that?" she asked, white-faced and stunned. "Tommy, do you remember where that was taken? Do you have the address?"

Tom, Jr. looked at his mother's best friend, startled. "Yes, of course I do. But I thought you already knew where…"

Before Tommy could finish his sentence, Kate was wrapping her arms around him in the tightest hug imaginable.

°°°

The next day, Kate flew to Paris. She always stayed at the Hotel Montalembert, located on the Left Bank, on a small street right off Rue du Bac. It was the perfect place for her, as they had small, intimate rooms, a tiny elevator that fit two at the most, and a very inviting dining room with a fireplace, where she had had many breakfast and lunch meetings in the last few years. The doorman knew her name, as did the sweet-faced waitress who served her breakfast. The Montalembert was just a short walk away from her other favorite place, Les Deux Magots, which was right in the heart of Saint-Germain-des-Prés. There, she could sit for hours, after all her meetings were done for the day. Undisturbed and happy as a lark, outside at a table of her own and, under the protection of an expansive green awning, she could watch hundreds of Parisians go by.

Kate had an appointment the morning after her arrival with one of the representatives of a well-known tannery in France. Luckily, it was a breakfast meeting, downstairs in the dining room. Dressed in a white silk blouse, black skirt and heels, she felt rested, but still wished she'd had another hour of sleep.

Just as she was about to go out the door, she glanced over at her suitcase, and without thinking, reached over to slip her hand into the side flap. Then, suddenly, mid-action, she stopped and tears came to her eyes. *It won't be there*, she thought to herself. *There are no more messages from him. He's gone.* Still, after all this time, sometimes she just forgot. Forgot that her father was gone, forgot that he was no longer with her. Forgot that when she called home, he would never be there to pick up the phone again. She opened the door, took a deep breath, looked back, and was about to head out when she did indeed see the very tip of a cream-colored envelope in the side flap of her suitcase. The kind of envelope her father used to use. Reaching over, she touched it and then—slowly, slowly—gently pulled it out.

°°°

The letter sat in her handbag all through the breakfast meeting. The representative of Tanneries Haas invited Kate to join him, at the end of the week, on a visit to the Alsatian village where the workshop was located. There, he explained, she could go through the different hides and pick out the ones she liked. Kate nodded and listened and examined the samples he provided her. They were magnificent, but she could barely see or feel a thing. All she could think about was her father's letter in her purse. She accepted the invitation to go to the Haas workshop. Normally she would have been over-the-moon excited by the prospect of going to the famed place. The fact was, though, she couldn't wait for the representative to leave and the meeting to be over, so she could read her letter.

The moment she was free, she decided not to go back upstairs to her room, but to go for a walk instead. *This will be my last letter from him*, she thought, as she left the hotel and turned the corner. *I want to treasure these moments before I open it, for as long as I can. He must have slipped it in knowing that it would be his final one.*

She walked down to the Seine, by the little green metal bookstalls along the way, and then across the bridge toward the Right Bank. She was headed to the address that her godson Tommy had given her, the picture he'd taken clutched in her hand.

There's nowhere you can be
that isn't where you're meant to be.
- John Lennon

CHAPTER NINETEEN

POPPY stood on the balcony in her long white nightgown, not believing her eyes. There, stretched out in front of her, was a place which, up until now, she had believed was just a figment of Lucienne Badeaux's imagination. It was a house of prayer that to Poppy was like heaven itself. This was the same church, the surrounding fields now long-gone, that was in her father's book, the same church in the painting she had treasured over the years, and the very same church that was the insignia in the only purse she ever carried now. She was utterly speechless. Backing into the room, she slid down onto the bed.

Staring up at the ceiling, she tried to make sense of it all. But what explanation could there be? Exhilarated, she quickly showered and dressed. Then, with great anticipation, grabbing her purse, she made her way down the three flights of stairs and out the door.

The inexplicable thing was, though she knew she had never been there before, everything was eerily familiar. She recognized old buildings here and there around the church that leaned this way and that. Some were stone, and some were half-timbered and whitewashed in the medieval style.

Upon entering the church, she glanced around. Even before she set eyes on them, she knew that there would be eight stained glass windows, two above the main altar, and six along the walls. She breathed in the smell of the candles blazing at the various tiny altars to saints along the sides. Their scent filled her with enormous pleasure and peace.

Poppy couldn't help noticing a statue of St. Anthony in an alcove to the side. She made her way over. Surrounding the statue were candles, many of them lit and glittering brightly. She'd been praying to him daily since the first time she turned to him for help in New York. Just as she lit a candle for Luna, the one she had lost, as she had hundreds of times before, the church door opened. Behind her, she felt a gentle draft of wind and heard the clicking of heels. A second later, a woman passed by, slid into a nearby pew, and knelt down.

Be still my heart.
Thou hast known worse than this.

- Homer

CHAPTER TWENTY

KATE knew this was the place the moment she turned the corner and set eyes on it. She let out a gasp. She was standing in the middle of a small area of Paris she had never been to before, washed in brilliant sunlight. Directly before her was the winding cobblestone street and the church with a single steeple, a sight she knew so well. Seeing this place that was so deeply ingrained in both her mind and heart was more overpowering than she had expected.

Collecting herself, she walked up the front steps, opened the door, and went in. It was a small, stone church, little more than a chapel, really, with eight delicate stained glass windows situated along the sides and behind the altar. It was empty except for one other person off to the side. Finding a pew, she genuflected, blessed herself, knelt down, and began to pray. After a few minutes, she sat back. With great tenderness, she reached into her purse for the envelope. Inside it, she found a letter and an old, tattered Polaroid picture. First, she took out the letter.

My dearest daughter,

Do you remember the year you and I built the life-size dollhouse in the backyard for Alice and Gwen? From March to May, we dedicated every Saturday morning to recreating a miniature replica of a house the girls had seen in a magazine. It was in between the sawing, hammering, hoisting, and painting that I had planned to tell you. But the moment never seemed right, and so the words never came.

Years went by and one missed opportunity turned into two, then three, then four.

I'm sorry for waiting so long to tell you something you always had the right to know. I'm sorry for not admitting the truth when you asked me as a child—I was so afraid you would never trust me again.

I am your real father, your mother was your real mother, but we were unable to conceive a child, which is why we adopted you.

The woman who gave birth to you was nineteen and unmarried. She wanted a better life for her child. And we just wanted... you.

I hope you will forgive me. I love you, my darling daughter. You are the light of my life.

Always,
Dad

The Kingdom of Heaven is not a place,
but a state of mind.
- John Burroughs

CHAPTER TWENTY-ONE

THE SOUNDS she heard splintered her heart. At first, Poppy thought it was the moaning of the old church, after centuries, still settling in. But as moments passed, she found the sounds to be of a more serious and desperate nature. For reasons she could not comprehend, she felt the agony as if it were her own. She slid into the pew in which the woman wept, and knelt down.

Something about this woman's slender, trembling body begged to be held. It was crazy, Poppy knew, but she could not fight the need to console. Tentatively, she reached out and put her arm around the woman's shoulders. She was afraid that such an intimate act would be startling, but the woman did not seem to mind. In fact, now that she was being held, she simply wept harder.

"Shh," Poppy whispered. "It's going to be okay."

The woman looked up, surprised to hear English spoken. Their eyes met.

"You're American?" the woman managed to whisper through sobs. "I know I'm making a fool of myself. Please forgive me."

Her voice... It stirred something in Poppy. She handed the woman a handkerchief.

The woman took it gladly. "Thank you. You're so kind. It really is wonderful when a perfect stranger suddenly appears at just the right time."

As they both descended the church steps a little while later, side-by-side, a cool, late morning breeze gently blew by.

"You won't believe this," Poppy confided in the woman. "But I've had a painting of this church since I was a girl. My father found it for me."

The woman turned to her, staring in amazement. "*You* won't believe this either, but I've had a painting of the church for a long time, too. Though it's only a copy. I cherish it so much, in fact, that I actually use it as a logo for my company."

Poppy's eyes focused for the first time on the leather purse hanging from the woman's shoulder.

Breathlessly, she blurted, "I know you, I think. Are you Kate Kennedy?"

A bit taken aback, Kate admitted that she was.

"Look, I have one of your purses," Poppy cried with elation as she held it out for Kate to see. "I love it. In fact, it's one of my most prized possessions."

"That's unbelievable. It really is. I'm so flattered. And may I ask what *you* do?"

"I write. I'm a writer."

"Oh really, anything I might know?"

"Maybe. Have you heard of the *Luna* series?"

Kate's hand flew to her mouth.

"You're P.R. Doumas? That's how I know you! The minute I saw you I felt like I'd seen you somewhere before."

The two of them decided to find a place to have a cup of tea.

"Are you feeling a little better?" Poppy asked, when they found a small café with a geranium-red awning, its name, La Clé, spelled out across the front.

"I just learned something very painful today," Kate told Poppy, her large brown eyes turning away to conceal her pain. "It's all so new to me that I don't think I can talk about it yet."

"Then don't," Poppy agreed, patting her hand.

Not all who wander are lost.

-J.R.R. Tolkien

CHAPTER TWENTY-TWO

POPPY and Kate had almost a week together in Paris. When Kate wasn't in meetings she joined Poppy, and the two of them spent their days strolling and talking.

"I know it sounds strange," Kate had said the day they had agreed to first meet up. "But it seems like I've known you forever, somehow."

"I know," Poppy agreed. "I feel the same way. Usually I like wandering around on my own. But wandering with you is even better."

They sailed boats in a pond at the Jardin du Luxembourg, laughing when two pigeons landed on Poppy's boat to take a free ride. Then they lunched on baguettes oozing with brie, on a bench in the Jardin des Tuileries.

The following day they took the Métro to Boulogne-Billancourt, to the Albert Kahn Museum, where they delighted in ten acres of luscious gardens. Winding paths led them through meadows of flowers growing wild and free. There were some stepping stones that led across a shallow pond that held glimmering red and gold koi, who sucked pleasantly on their fingertips when they dipped them in. They asked a stranger to take a picture of them standing on an exquisite Japanese arched bridge that crossed a larger pond bursting with lilies.

It was there that Kate noticed a father and his little girl strolling by. Without warning, tears welled up in her eyes and streamed down her cheeks. Poppy reached out and took her hand, leading her quietly to a wood of willows nearby, where they could talk privately.

"I found a letter from my late father..." Kate explained. "He had tucked it into my suitcase before he died." She stopped for a moment and smiled wistfully. "He did that kind of thing when I traveled... left me notes, wishing me a good day. I held on to this one, not wanting to open it right away, knowing it would be the last one I would ever receive."

Poppy squeezed Kate's hand. The sun was bright that day, and as they walked, it streamed down through the branches, making puddles of warm, buttery light along the way.

"But when I finally did open it in the church, that day we met, I saw that it was not a note at all," Kate continued. "It was a letter in which he wrote that he and my mother had adopted me when they found they couldn't conceive. He said that he knew he should have told me while I was growing up, but it seemed there was never a good time. And I understand that—because I understood him—but I wish he had been able to tell me, because at least I could have asked him all the questions I have now. And I have so many. "

◦◦◦

They never grew tired of hearing each other's accounts

of their lives. In the Rodin Museum, as they were wandering around, Poppy told Kate about Beatrice and Peter, and that Ari was in Prague directing the last of the *Luna* movies, and had banished her from the set for the first two weeks. She also talked about how despondent she had felt after writing the final book.

"Did you stop because Luna grew up?" asked Kate.

"Yes, and also because my reason for writing them, my dream and my hope for what they might bring me, was never realized."

"And what was that?" Kate questioned.

Poppy shook her head. "Oh, it's a long story," she said. "It's much like yours, but in reverse."

As they were winding their way back out of the museum grounds, they came upon the famous sculpture called *The Burghers of Calais*, which they hadn't noticed on their way in. Kate stopped suddenly. "Oh my goodness," she said. "Isn't this incredible? Look at the pain on their faces. Look at that one," she pointed. "He looks so torn, doesn't he?" Poppy stood beside her, studying the sculpture of the six would-be martyrs of Calais. "Do you know the story behind this?" Poppy asked her. "Yes," Kate smiled. "It was one of my father's favorite stories. He first told it to me years and years ago."

°°°

Over tea, Kate told Poppy about desperately wanting to be a nun, falling in love with Scott, and going to Lourdes to pray. "Funny thing was," she said, laughing, "I never actually made a decision in Lourdes, after all that. I made it just before I bought the painting of the church we both love... here in Paris... somewhere around Notre Dame."

By the fourth day, the day before Kate was to leave for the tannery, she and Poppy found themselves mostly outside, despite the occasional rain. When the skies opened, they huddled under a giant umbrella Poppy found in the apartment she was staying in. They walked along the Seine and waved at people on the boats. They wandered up and down the cobbled streets, looking in shop windows, but never buying a thing. It wasn't until they were overcome by the frenzy of scents at Marché Monge, an open-air food market, that they were enticed to go on their first shopping spree. They perused dozens of crowded stalls, and picked out herbs of all kinds; fresh potatoes, carrots and onions, all packed in good, brown earth; lamb pieces; a newly-baked, crisp loaf of bread; some cuts of cheese and a bottle of Bordeaux. Struggling under the weight of their packages on the Métro, they finally arrived at Poppy's apartment, exhausted but excited. There, they began to chop and cook and sip the wine, as they sang along with Edith Piaf to "Non, Je Ne Regrette Rien" at the top of their lungs, over and over again.

"This is the way we should always live," Kate said, pouring each of them another glass of wine and lighting the candles. Poppy clinked her glass with Kate's in agreement.

The table was set right by the balcony. Through the open French doors, they could see their church, the church that was so dear to each of them.

◦◦◦

"I was a girl, just nineteen, when I fell in love for the very first time," Poppy told Kate over dinner. "I had a baby, a daughter, but I had to give her up." She stopped, looked down at her hands, then continued on. "It turned out that he was married and hadn't told me. Before the nurses took my baby away, I was allowed to see her for only a few moments. I will never forget the feeling of love that pierced straight through me when I looked at her face. She had the most beautiful brown eyes I had ever seen—eyes that looked at me with perfect trust." She took a deep breath, held it for a moment, and let it out in a slow sigh.

"Half a year later, I married her father," Poppy went on. "It turned out he'd been in the process of getting a divorce, leaving an arranged marriage, in fact. We tried to search for our daughter, but because it was a closed adoption, the law prevented us from finding any information whatsoever. I was so afraid that something terrible had happened to her. That she wasn't being cared for properly. Or even worse, that she had died. It was like she had vanished into thin air. Disappeared off the face of the earth. So the *Luna* books were my only way of keeping her with me. My only way of having her back. My only way to watch her grow."

"That's sad, and yet so beautiful," Kate said. "It really is the reverse of my story, and I hope with all my heart that you find each other one day."

Fate chooses our relatives;
we choose our friends.
- Jacques Delille

CHAPTER TWENTY-THREE

KATE had her bag packed and was having breakfast with Poppy at the outdoor café attached to her hotel. A brisk breeze was blowing, and the awning shading them made a soft flapping noise, like the sound of a playing card wedged into the spokes of a wheel. In less than twenty minutes, the representative from Tanneries Haas was going to be picking her up and driving her to the Haas family's two-hundred-year-old workshop. Although she was happy about driving through the French countryside and visiting the renowned facility, she was equally unhappy about parting company with Poppy. Despite the terrible circumstance, their chance encounter in the church five days ago had turned out to be an unexpected gift for both of them. Of course, they would keep in touch. Their days in Paris had been unhurried and tranquil, but with them both being so busy, who knew when they would be able to see one another again. A perfect week, they had decided. One of the most perfect weeks either could remember having in years—a week of just wandering and talking, a week of getting to know a perfect stranger and growing to love someone new. To think that Kate had been dreading this trip!

"I'm going to miss our time together," Kate was telling Poppy, when the sweet waitress she liked so much set a small pot of jam on the table. A wide smile on the waitress's face, she told Kate, "Votre mère est très belle, comme vous."

They both laughed happily, but shook their heads, Kate adding, "No, madame, she is not my mother—she is just a dear friend."

"While we are on the subject," Poppy began, as she dipped into the strawberry jam and spread it out evenly on her toast, "do you think you will search for your birth mother someday? Or is it all too new to even think about yet?"

The breeze was picking up, turning, in fact, into something more vigorous, forcing Kate to grab her napkin just as it started to fly away. "After your story last night," she said, safely tucking the napkin under her purse, "of searching for your daughter for years, it occurred to me that... my mother—my birth mother, that is—might be wanting to find me, too. So I thought I might ask you for some advice. But first I want to show you something I neglected to mention before. It's a picture that I'm uncertain what to do with."

Reaching down into her suitcase, she carefully slipped out her father's envelope and removed the Polaroid picture from inside. "When I saw it, I was very confused. It's a picture of me from when I was six, standing between two women. I remember when it was taken. I was at school, and they had handed their camera to someone so the two of them could be in the picture with me. It wasn't until after your story that I began to consider that maybe my father put it in his letter because these women knew something about my birth."

As it sometimes happens, the brisk breeze that had turned into something more impatient, suddenly now changed yet again. And with no notice at all, a wily and outrageous wind came swooping in, snatching hats off heads and scarves off necks, tossing and twirling them around. The wind tipped over empty tables and stripped some of the umbrellas from their heavy stands. Chairs went clanking to the ground. Long, white nightgowns from a drying line belonging to a cloister of nuns nearby, took off and, like a graceful rapture of snowy eagles, soared high before escaping, ghostlike, over rooftops and out of sight. The unpredictable wind raged so hard that Poppy and Kate's hair blew madly around their heads. And that's when Poppy saw Kate's Polaroid picture fly out of her hand. And on a taunting gust, it wafted briefly, hovered, lingered momentarily, just above them, just out of reach, and then, spiraling like a whirling dervish, it took wing and flew away.

"Oh my dear God," Kate screamed, frozen in place.

But Poppy rose instantly and sprinted after it, running as fast as she could in an attempt to keep her eyes focused on it, as it coasted this way and that. She tracked it across Rue de Montalembert and then, picking up her pace, she followed it as it twisted right down Rue du Bac, then zigzagged towards the swiftly-flowing Seine. The traffic on the *quai* was speeding by, and as the picture floated over tops of cars, Poppy raced, weaving in and out, ignoring the honking horns. Just as she was nearly below the photograph, her arms outstretched, a great gust cruelly swirled it even higher and sent it flying over a wall, close to the river's edge. It was a dapper gentleman well into his nineties, wearing a paisley cravat that whipped wildly around his neck, who reached up and plucked it effortlessly out of the sky.

"Oh merci, monsieur, thank you very, very much," Poppy screamed with relief.

"Mon plaisir." The gentleman bowed, and then vanished.

Returning the way she'd come, or thought she had come, Poppy raced down one wrong street after another, finally noticing that everything looked so different because all of the outdoor cafés along the way had taken in their tables and chairs and closed their doors. It was close to twenty minutes later when she found her way back to the hotel café, out of breath. Everything was cleared away there, too. The tables, chairs, umbrellas were gone, and the wooden doors closed and locked up. Finding the hotel entrance, she went into the lobby and looked around for Kate.

A doorman smiled and handed her a note.

Dear Poppy,

I ran after you but I couldn't find you, you disappeared so fast. Now the representative from the tannery is here and there is no place for him to park. I want to wait for you but I think I may be forced to go. I am devastated that I can't hug you goodbye.

Thank you for trying to save my picture. Now, with it gone, I guess I will never know about my birth mother, as it was my only clue.

Goodbye for now, until we meet again.

Your loving friend,
Kate

∘ ∘ ∘

Poppy was disappointed that she had missed Kate, but she would be eternally grateful that she had rescued the Polaroid. For when she set eyes on the small photograph, she recognized immediately the two women in it, and, in a state of utter disbelief, she called them without delay.

Find a place inside where there's joy,
and the joy will burn out the pain.
- Joseph Campbell

CHAPTER TWENTY-FOUR

"W H A T goes around comes around," Jewell said, shaking her head, piled high with white, silky hair.

"No, that's not the way it goes. It's 'what comes around, goes around.'" Jane laughed, her own silky white hair piled up in the same fashion.

The only difference between the two sisters now was that Jane was thirty pounds heavier, carried a cane and wore sneakers. Jewell, on the other hand, had kept her figure, did Pilates daily, and still wore heels as high as she could manage without falling and breaking her neck.

After both of their husbands had passed away, they had moved in together. They had had to draw a card to determine whose house, out of the two, would be the one to be sold. Jane had won. She was thrilled to move into Jewell's, which had been the house they grew up in, after all, and where there was air-conditioning and internet access, too.

They had long ago stopped writing their cookbooks. The ones that they had written, though, now sold on eBay. In fact, if they were signed by both, they sold for hundreds of dollars, which made them laugh.

Jane had taken over Poppy's room. It was large, with windows that looked out over the pastures, up the hills, and even into the woods beyond. She and her sister didn't climb up to those woods anymore. They had stopped walking together recently, after Jane sprained her ankle one day when she stepped into a rabbit hole. She went around bandaged up now, totally dependent on her cane.

Jewell called her an old gimp. She didn't mind. It finally gave her an excuse not to attend cocktail parties, garden club meetings, and the like. She could actually do what she wanted now. And that was to get on her iPad and read e-books and newspapers from around the world, all day.

Jewell, on the other hand, was as fiery as ever, out and about as much as she could be, returning home with stories to regale her sister with, forcing her to put down everything and listen.

"Elizabeth Page's granddaughter was expelled from Andover for going to a few classes drunk as a skunk," Jewell reported as she threw off her heels and poured herself a gin and tonic.

"They call it *hooking up* now, you know," she told her sister as she fell into her chair near the fireplace. "It sounds so unromantic. Like a bunch of trucks getting together, don't you think? And, oh yes," she went on, without skipping a beat, "it seems that you can now talk someone into committing suicide on Facebook and get away with it. Apparently Margo Pew's great nephew..."

When the telephone rang neither of them wanted to get up to answer it. Finally, Jane pulled herself out of her over-stuffed chair and went over. By then though, it had passed on to voicemail.

"Hello," a stern voice said. "It's me. I need to talk to you. The two of you. Together. I'll be there tomorrow afternoon. So please be home."

Jane returned to her chair and sat down. The two of them remained quiet for a long while. Then, Jewell finished off her drink and set the glass down.

"I wonder what that's all about," she said.

Shrugging her shoulders, Jane tilted her old, gray head. "Something important, I would say."

Jewell looked up and smiled. "Yes. We haven't seen her in a while."

Jane noticed that after her sister turned away, Jewell's eyes were alight with tears. In all the years of their life together, she had never seen Jewell cry over anything. She had turned red with fury, shrieked, yelled and screamed, beat her fists on the table, but she had never shed a real, genuine tear. Jewell's tears now made Jane sit up and take notice. Unexpectedly, her sister was unmasked and vulnerable.

How the tables had turned. Jane had never realized Jewell cared about her daughter so much. It had been Jane who cared about Poppy all these years. This new Jewell was a surprise to her. She wasn't sure what to do. Should she go over and try and comfort her, or allow her to be alone for a while? Let her reflect on things she had never allowed herself to feel before. Or possibly it wasn't that at all, it occurred to Jane out of the blue. Maybe Jewell was not sad, but frightened. In fact, Jane thought it was more likely that she was terrified Poppy had found out that they had known where Kate had been all these years and had kept it from her.

Maybe now was the moment, Jane considered. She had never divulged to Jewell that Poppy's baby had a heart murmur. And she certainly hadn't told her about what she and Father Sean Patrick had planned so many years ago. It would be such a relief to be able to finally let it out.

As she watched her sister, she was surprised that Jewell was not even bothering to wipe away her tears. She just let them flow and flow and flow. This sister of hers, this girl, this woman, this old lady, had had everything her entire life. While she, Jane, the good and kind sister, the benevolent sister, had been left empty-handed in so many ways. Jane had had no true partner in life. Fitz had been a hopeless, good-for-nothing, who cared about nobody but himself and his horses and fox hunting. Everyone thought he was such a stud, so handsome, prancing around like he was a movie star or something. Sadly, they had been unable to produce a baby. A baby of their own. *Her* own. A baby she could cuddle in her arms, nurse as she fell off to sleep. A baby she could name. Grace, she would have called her. Rose Grace would have been her name if she had been a daughter. And she would have been. Jane knew that for an absolute fact.

Jewell's daughter had loved Jane best. Jane knew that for an absolute fact, also. She clearly remembered, as though it had been just yesterday, taking the little infant Poppy from the doctor's arms the second after she was born. She distinctly recalled breathing in the first scent of her tiny niece. How sweet it had been, like a clear summer's day. A scent Jewell had never seemed to notice or appreciate when Jane had tried to talk to her about it.

"What are you going on about?" her sister had said. "She smells like a baby, nothing more." Jane had loathed her sister for not loving her baby passionately from the moment she was born. But somehow, she had not been surprised. Jewell had never loved anyone except herself. Not even her. Plain Janey, she had called her. Yes, they had been identical twins and had looked exactly alike since birth. But the day Jewell could utter her first sentence at the age of a year and a half, she had nicknamed her Plain Janey.

Plain Janey, indeed, Jane thought to herself. At least their mother had put an end to that by the time they were four. Everyone knew she was certainly the kinder and more caring of the two. Yes, she had been shy. Reclusive. Withdrawn. But there was no other position for her in the family, what with Jewell being so vivacious and entertaining. *Delightfully delicious* is what the first grade teacher had called Jewell. Delightfully delicious! What was Jane, a bowl of hogwash? She remembered how the teacher's words had made her feel. They had crushed her and made her angry and hurt for the entire school year.

I want her to read my diaries, she decided suddenly. She didn't want to die someday without having seen Jewell's face as she learned that Jane had been strong, too. That she had a world of her own, apart from her sister's. That she could have been the *delightfully delicious* one if she hadn't been forced to live in Jewell's shadow. That she had been capable of being in the world without Jewell beside her. That she, Jane, was worthy of respect and admiration, too.

Love is my religion—
I could die for it.
- John Keats

CHAPTER TWENTY-FIVE

THAT NIGHT in bed, a little past three a.m., just as Jewell was finishing the last of Jane's diaries, her room strewn with red leather books, she suddenly felt her chest tighten. She hadn't understood at first why Jane had asked her to read her diaries. But now that she was finished, a strange peace had come over her. Jane's account of her years had given Jewell a new understanding of the person closest to her in the world, a person so familiar, and yet now seen as if for the first time.

Her head began to swim, memories appearing and disappearing, until her mind focused on one in particular.

It was one of her and her sister when they were very young—seven, she thought. Or was it eight? They had begged their mother to allow them to fetch the milk from the little farmhouse down the way. The snow was newly-fallen, everything for miles was white and clean, and they delighted in making the first footprints in it that early morning. Jewell remembered it so vividly, as if it were happening to her just then, one of her favorite things, seeing her tracks alongside Jane's, as though they were a four-footed girl. When they arrived at the house, one of the glistening icicles hanging from the porch roof snapped and shattered on the ground. "It's like a handful of fairy dust," Jane said, as they knocked on the door.

"Oh dear me, hello there, girls," Mrs. Kane's gentle voice called out, her tiny, century-old face crisscrossed with lines, her eyes beaming happily. The scent of dried herbs hanging along the rafters in thick bunches and the warmth from the fire felt good as they were ushered in. It was a one-room cottage with not much in it. A single wrought-iron bed stood against one wall, covered in heaps of quilts all made from neat squares of dresses Mrs. Kane had worn through her years. A black, metal coal stove stood against another wall, and a chipped farmhouse sink stood against another. In the center was a simple table with a bowl of dried wildflowers, and a single chair with an old crimson cushion. The small, homey place was immaculate; the dirt floor, Jewell noticed from the newly-made marks across it, had just been swept clean.

"How many cans today?" Mrs. Kane asked, as she shuffled off in a timeworn pair of slippers to the far end of the room.

"One for each of us, please," they answered in unison, waiting impatiently for what would happen next.

With the flamboyancy of a stage magician, Mrs. Kane drew back a faded old curtain, exposing the rest of the room. And there stood Daisy, the cow, beneath a snow covered window, chewing on a pile of hay. Without a word, Mrs. Kane pulled over her three-legged stool and began to milk into a basin she held in her lap.

Just as Mrs. Kane was leaning over to give her and Jane a taste of the thick cream she ladled from the top, the memory faded away, and Jewell felt a terrible pain in her chest, where the tightness had been. It was a hurt so sharp and excruciating that she was forced to suck in a weak breath, and struggle to call out one single name.

"Jane!" she cried. "Jaaaaaaaaaaaane," she cried out again, for all she was worth. But there was no answer, at least not one she heard.

○○○

Jane had gone to bed with some anxiety, knowing that her sister was up, reading her diaries. Now in her sleep, she heard her name being called as if by the wind. She sat up abruptly. Then she heard it again. Pulling her covers aside, she moved as fast as she could on her sprained ankle, through her room, then out into the hall. Jewell's room was just across the way.

She saw that Jewell had gotten through them all. And she felt such peace at that. Then she looked over at Jewell herself. She was not moving. She was on her back, staring up at the ceiling. Her sister was dead. She fell across Jewell's body and tried to shake her alive. She put her mouth on Jewell's lips and desperately attempted to blow in life. She pumped Jewell's heart frantically, urgently, feverishly with the palms of both hands. "Don't leave me, Jewell," she cried, tears splashing out from her old, worn eyes. "Don't leave me here all alone," she pleaded, lying beside Jewell and hugging her close. "You are the dearest person in the world to me, no matter what you said or did, I will always love you. Please take me with you, Jewell," she howled, terrified, into the lonely dark of the night.

∞

She was about to spread her arms, when suddenly she heard a whimpering cry, an insistent whine. Reluctantly, she reached back to where she had just come from. Feeling the pulse of her sister's hand, she gripped it tightly and pulled, until it was as light and free as she.

A wounded deer leaps the highest.
- Emily Dickinson

CHAPTER TWENTY-SIX

SHE HEARD the humming, the soft silky sound, that in eras long past, before speech, was a form of communication among kin.

It was a mellifluous, comforting sound, Kate thought, having heard it sometime before.

○○○

Poppy did not hear the humming. She was racing too fast out of the airport to hear anything but the beat of her own heart, thundering inside.

Glistening shards, thickets of splinters, all fragments of disregarded memories, had begun to merge into a shape in her mind. Events she could never have fathomed, even in her wildest dreams, were becoming truths. And the only two people who held all the pieces to this gargantuan puzzle created over years and years, were now only an hour's drive away.

∞

"Where are we?" they asked.

"It will return to you," was the reply. "You are back. You are home. Don't worry," the guardians reassured them. "Soon you will remember it all again."

Every day is a journey,
and the journey itself is home.
- Matsuo Bashō

CHAPTER TWENTY-SEVEN

POPPY sped down the driveway. As she slammed on the brakes in front of the house, the dirt scattered and danced beneath her tires.

She smashed the knocker against the front door, and it came off in her hand.

"I know you are in there," she screamed out angrily. "I'm coming in." She flung open the rickety door.

She moved quickly from room to room. "How dare you try and hide from me," she screamed.

"Where are you two?" she shouted. She ran up the stairs two at a time. "I called you. I warned you. I left a message. You knew I'd be here."

It was in her mother's room that she found them at last. There they were, side-by-side, fast asleep on the bed.

"Wake up," she screamed. "Wake up. I'm here."

They did not stir. Then words began to pour out of Poppy.

"How dare you pretend to be asleep? Open your eyes,"

she yelled. "I want to look into them when you tell me, face to face, what you did. After all these years I want the truth. You stole her from me, didn't you? You knew all along where she was."

Tears began rolling uncontrollably from her eyes.

"Did you think that by hiding her away you were protecting me somehow? It was you two that I needed to be protected from. You always had each other. I had no one. And when I finally had her, you did everything you could to separate me from her. How could you do that? How could you have spent all those years, knowing exactly where she was, while I yearned for her, not knowing if she was dead or alive? You met her without telling me. I have proof of that meeting. I have a picture."

A perfect silence followed. As she looked down at their unmoving bodies, she finally understood that they were dead. And she finally noticed all the red diaries scattered around the room. She heard the hum then, the hum that encircled her and clung to her like a wet sheet. A great sorrow overtook her. And she covered her face with her hands and let out a moan.

More than anything else, she yearned to cross the room and curl up between them on the bed, just for a little while.

$$\infty$$

They looked in, two leaves clinging to a windowpane. They saw the deserted figure of their beloved girl, grieving for them. They wanted so badly to take her anguish away. "We are none of us ever alone," came the whisper again. "We are all linked, attached, a part of one another. Whether we know it or not."

We will only understand the miracle of life fully,
when we allow the unexpected to happen.
- Paulo Coelho

CHAPTER TWENTY-EIGHT

AFTER the bodies were taken away, the paramedics had gone, and the house was empty at last, she came back into the bedroom. It was only now that she saw them. All the faces she knew. Faces in frames. There were sterling silver frames everywhere, on every dresser, every table, many on either side of her mother's bed. Frames of all sizes and shapes. Frames old and new. There were frames with photographs of her father, her mother, her aunt, herself, as babies, as adolescents, as adults, all smiling, happy, with not a care in the world. There were pictures of her children, Beatrice and Peter, and there were even several of her and Ari.

And then she saw, among the many frames, a group of pictures of someone she didn't know. There was a picture of a toddler at the seashore, laughing and running through the waves. There was a picture of the same face in a first Holy Communion dress, smiling joyfully, and even more of the same child grown up, winning a prize of some kind, and going off to a prom. Another photo, a smaller one, hidden behind the others, was of the same little girl, only this time without her two front teeth. And standing with her, on either side, were her mother and her aunt Jane. It was the same picture, she realized with a start, as the one she had run after in the streets of Paris. Suddenly it flashed through Poppy's mind, like the quick snap of a serpent's tail, that her mother and aunt hadn't just met her once, but had known her daughter her entire life. It seemed that they had loved her, too.

∞

Everything was right. Everything was in order. The moon, the sun, the stars, all rested. The winds hesitated and the waters went still.

They were no longer of an age. They were of all time, yet again.

In three words I can sum up everything
I've learned about life:
It goes on.
- Robert Frost

CHAPTER TWENTY-NINE

THE MAID at the Hotel Montalembert who had come in with Kate's breakfast brought several American newspapers with her. Kate thanked her profusely, and as she drank her first cup of coffee she spread out *The New York Times* to catch up on the news she had missed. She had stayed a few days longer than planned at Tanneries Haas. They had been wonderful with her, kind and patient, complimenting her sketches and suggesting various combinations of leathers and colors that she could mix into her designs. It had been an exhilarating time, and she had worked hard and long each day. Now, in the late afternoon, back in Paris, she had woken up to find that she'd slept most of the day away. Rather than chide herself for the lost time, she'd decided to be grateful for the rest and had ordered breakfast for dinner.

She missed Poppy. She would have loved to have had dinner with her that night and tell her about her time at the tannery. The night before, when she returned, she'd been given a note that Poppy had left behind. It informed her that Poppy had an emergency back in the States and needed to leave immediately. It continued:

But I found your picture. A nice man literally grabbed it out of the wind. It is enclosed safely in this envelope, along with my love.

Until we speak again, au revoir, ma chére amie.

Poppy

Pouring herself a second cup of coffee and taking a bite of croissant, Kate was just finishing the business section, when suddenly something she saw took her breath away. Warily, she set down her coffee cup and stared down at the picture and words in front of her.

Famous Twins, Jewell Penrose Russell and Jane Penrose Perkins, Co-Authors of Beloved Cookbooks, Dead at 86

Jewell Penrose Russell and Jane Penrose Perkins, twin sisters and famous Main Line debutantes, who often appeared on the social pages of The Philadelphia Inquirer *and* The Philadelphia Bulletin, *as well as in many well-known magazines such as* Town and Country *and* Life, *died of natural causes, apparently simultaneously, on Tuesday, May 17th, at Sunny Brook Farm, the home they shared, in Chester Springs, PA.*

"Their lives were always intertwined," Poppy Russell Doumas, author of the popular Luna *series and*

daughter and niece to the deceased, told the Times. *"It's only fitting that they left this world together, hand in hand."*

Kate stopped reading and quickly turned her eyes to the picture, not believing what she saw. Her hands were trembling. It was of two beautiful women in their 40s, dressed smartly, each wearing a pearl necklace, and a radiant, perfect smile. They looked to be the very same women who had long ago posed with her for the picture Poppy had returned, and that lay in the envelope on the desk across from her bed. Stunned, she rose shakily, grabbed the envelope, took the picture out, and held it next to the photograph in the paper.

And then, like a swift, unexpected blow to the chest, it came to her. Clear as a shrill whistle through the hush of the night. There was no doubt in her mind about who these women were. She had been aware of them off and on almost all of her childhood.

Searching her purse for her phone, she scrolled down her list of contacts, and stopped when she reached the name she wanted.

There was no answer. She left a voicemail.

"Hello Poppy," she said. "This is Kate. I just saw the obituary in the *Times*. I'm very sorry for your loss, but I think we need to talk right away."

Her hand was trembling so hard that it took her several attempts to hang up.

As she leaned on the desk for support, out of nowhere it seemed, she began to feel a sense of having been violated.

Grief can be the garden of compassion.

- Rumi

CHAPTER THIRTY

W H E N Poppy's cell phone trilled, they were driving to the funeral home to make arrangements. Ari was beside her in the passenger seat, Beatrice and Peter behind them. It had been so many years since the four of them had been alone together like this. Mother and father in front, the two children in the back seat.

The funeral home was very close to The Church of the Holy Apostles on Pennswood Road in Bryn Mawr, where five generations of Penroses had been baptized and laid to rest. Although it was clearly marked on the map they had downloaded, it was nowhere to be seen on Pennswood Road, through the thick rows of trees. They had already been forced to make several U-turns in search of the place.

Poppy's purse was in the back, so Beatrice grabbed it and, without a word, took out the cell phone that had just stopped ringing. She listened to the voice message.

"It's from someone called Kate. She read the obituary and needs to talk to you right away," she told her mother. "Who's Kate, Mom?" she asked.

Poppy turned and looked at Ari. He reached over and

gave her shoulder a gentle squeeze. She pulled the car to the side of the road and took the keys out of the ignition. And then, with long heavy heaves, she began to cry.

"I found her," she told Beatrice and Peter between sobs. "I found your sister by accident while I was in Paris."

○○○

The first person Poppy had called when she had found the bodies was Ari, in Prague. He had just been getting ready to go off to the set.

"What are you doing in Philadelphia?" he'd asked, alarmed. "Yesterday you were in Paris."

Slowly, carefully, tearfully she had told him everything that had happened. "I found Luna, Ari. In the church from my painting. It's a long story, I'll tell you in detail later, but she showed me a picture of herself taken when she was six. And my mother and aunt were standing with her, in front of her school. They knew all along where she was, Ari, and never said a word to me. I was so furious at them when I found out... so mad and hurt... that I wanted to strangle them both. And then when I arrived here..."

"Oh God, Poppy, I wish I was there with you. You don't have to cope with this all by yourself. I'm getting on a plane right now, Sweetheart. I'm coming right away."

"I'm so glad, Ari. I need you here. And we'll be together when we tell Beatrice and Peter about Kate," Poppy said.

"Who's Kate?"

"Our Luna, Ari. Our Luna is now our Kate."

○○○

After the four of them had found the funeral home and the services were arranged, they stopped for breakfast.

161

Not a fancy place, but a place they were all familiar with—Teddy's, along Route 202.

"Shall we invite... Kate... to Grandmother and Great-Aunt Jane's funeral?" was the first question asked when they had ordered at the counter and all sat down in a red plastic booth. Teddy served comfort food, food that was satisfying, food that filled you up when you were starving or felt hollow inside. They sat in silence until their meals came. And as they ate, it was decided that Poppy would call Kate when they got home.

But Poppy couldn't eat a bite, she was so nervous. "I can't wait," she said, and after a few seconds she simply slipped out of the booth and went to the parking lot to call from there. On the first ring, her heart skipped a beat. On the second, she felt like she was going to throw up. On the third ring, her hands were shaking so much she was about to hang up—then Kate answered.

"Poppy?"

"Kate?" Poppy replied in barely a whisper.

"You're my mother, aren't you?" Kate came right out and said it.

Poppy's knees began to quake, and she felt like she was going to faint. Turning her back to the three faces staring at her through Teddy's sprawling window, she leaned against the side of the car for support. The day was overcast. Storm clouds were crowding in.

"Yes, I am your mother," she responded, just as the first drop of rain hit.

ooo

"She does not want to come to the funeral," Poppy told

Ari, Beatrice and Peter, when she walked back into Teddy's and slid into the booth. Her hands were still shaking, and Ari reached down to take them in his.

"She said she would feel peculiar being here," she recounted with tears in her eyes. "That maybe this was not a good time. Not the right time... for us all to meet."

ᵒᵒᵒ

The second time Poppy and Kate spoke, it was several days later. Ari had returned to Prague, and Beatrice had gone back to work. Peter had stayed behind to be with his mother a few days longer.

"Hello Kate, it's me, Poppy," she said.

There was a delicate pause before Kate finally said, "Hi."

The funeral had taken place by then. There had been a storm. The black umbrellas that had been passed out by the funeral home had been blown inside-out and torn to shreds. Many of the flower arrangements had scattered.

"Your two red roses were gorgeous, Kate. I put one on each of their coffins. It was a beautiful thing to send."

"Thank you. I didn't know what else to do. I didn't really know them. I just... saw them..." again, there was a slight hesitation, "a few times... you know."

Poppy picked up on Kate's cautious tone, which was very unlike her, or at least, not the Kate that she knew. "I understand. It was a difficult situation. They were strangers to you."

"Look, Poppy," Kate interrupted. "I'm so sorry. I need to tell you something—something that might be hard for you to hear. It's something I can't get out of my mind. I know this is a hard time for you. But, to be honest, I don't think I can put off telling you anymore."

Poppy held her breath. Then she asked, "What is it, Kate? Tell me."

"I don't believe we met in that church in Paris by accident like you made it seem," Kate said. "I don't think we met by chance at all. I don't think you just happened in and found me there. I don't know how you did it. But I suspect it was all planned. And I believe, like your mother and aunt, you knew all along where I was."

"No," Poppy tried to interject. "No, that's not true at all."

But Kate's firm voice overrode hers and went on.

"Maybe my birth came at an inconvenient time for you. Perhaps it was simpler to hand me off to someone and watch me from afar. It's obvious that you turned me into a character in a book to ease your guilt. But I am not Luna, Poppy. I am a real person. I have real emotions. I feel despair and happiness. I feel love and regret. I can also feel dishonored and violated. Stained. Soiled. Did it ever occur to you that I might not want you, Poppy? Did it ever occur to you that I might not want anything to do with you?"

"We need to talk, Kate. Face to face. I am flying down to see you. I am coming right away."

"No," Kate said. "I beg you, please. I don't want you to come."

Poppy could hear the panic in her voice. "All right," she whispered, trying desperately to stay calm. "I won't. But please, at least allow me to write to you. I don't understand any of this either. That I found you was a miracle, Kate. And miracles cannot be explained."

There is no greater agony
than bearing an untold story inside you.
- Maya Angelou

CHAPTER THIRTY-ONE

POPPY was in a panic. She didn't understand anything that was happening. It made no sense. No sense at all. She had found her daughter and was about to lose her again. The only two people who might have any answers were dead.

The night that Poppy got off the phone with Kate, Peter found his mother pacing up and down and around her office, unable to stop moving. It felt like she had to keep propelling herself forward until something, anything made sense.

He stood in the doorway, a cup of tea in hand.

"Mom? May I make a suggestion? When we were cleaning up in Granny's room, I packed away the diaries. They're in a box in the back of my car. How about I bring them up, and we can go through them together?"

Poppy thought for a moment. "Of course, the diaries! Good thinking, Peter!" she said. Maybe the diaries would explain how it was that Kate was in photographs all over her mother's bedroom. If she was ever going to have answers, surely they would be in her mother's diaries.

As Peter went downstairs and out to his car, she felt a growing sense of hope. She had no idea what was in the diaries. But there had to be something in them that would explain her mother's relationship to Kate.

°°°

The cup of tea Peter had brought up sat untouched and cold on her desk, as mother and son took turns scanning the pages and reading aloud to each other.

Poppy had realized immediately that this was not her mother's handwriting. This handwriting belonged to Aunt Jane. Her aunt's penmanship was beautiful to look at and easy to read. She knew it so well. It almost broke her heart to see it, the way every word tilted, shyly, to the left.

Peter read:

"He keeps calling for Poppy. Whenever Jewell hears his voice, she just hangs up. She grabs the phone anytime it rings, for fear Collier will pick up. God knows that would be a disaster. My brother-in-law's an old softie. He's likely to cave in and tell him exactly where to find Poppy at the convent. I listen in on the extension sometimes."

They turned page after page.

Poppy read next:

"Jewell and I met with Father Sean today. This whole thing just breaks my heart. It tears me apart. This baby, after all, is my

flesh and blood, too. Sometimes I have such doubts about all of this that I want to just curl up into a ball. But I have to force myself to be strong. I can't, I just can't be a part of Poppy keeping this child. It will ruin her life. All of my dreams for her... and of course her dreams for herself... will just wither away. I can't let that happen. It is our job to guide her toward the right path. She is so innocent, so trusting. Too gullible. She has no idea the true ways of the world. This man will not get a cent from our family if that's what he's after. He has no idea who he is up against. That is why I need to be there for her. Protect her. Keep him away. Father Sean has a family for the baby, he said. It's his nephew and his wife. We will meet them when he sees fit. The baby isn't due for another two months and..."

Poppy's eyes widened. They impatiently paged through the next diary.

"We met them today, the Doyles. Nellie is rather whimsical and thoughtful, and Franklyn seems confident and kind. It's obvious that they are elated about having this child. I completely approve of them and so does Jewell. She says they're normal. Stable. Ordinary... like she would know what normal was... They won't bring any unnecessary attention to themselves, she says. More importantly, they've agreed that Jewell and I can visit anytime we want, as long as we don't reveal who we are. Jewell says we shouldn't become too involved with the child. I agree. I just want to make sure she's safe and well taken care of. All I want is for her to be happy and..."

"The baby is born. She's a girl! When the doctor told Father Sean and me that she has a heart defect, we were shocked. Father Sean does not want to give the Doyles a sick child because they

don't have the money to care for her. He will make sure that the sick child, Poppy's child, goes to a wealthy family. But if she isn't adopted by his relatives, we won't have access to her. Jewell will never allow that. So I have to switch Poppy's baby with another, healthy one, and without Jewell knowing. At least this way, Jewell will feel like she has a connection with her granddaughter. And I will know that Poppy's baby is in good hands in a family with resources. All I have to do is take Poppy's baby and put her in another baby's crib, then switch wristbands. And figure out how to duplicate the birthmark on her chest."

Poppy took a deep breath and held it. Her heart beat hard and her body began to shake. She wanted all of this to go away, but she knew she had to keep reading. She felt Peter put his arm around her. And, with that, she became brave.

"Do you want me to continue reading, Mom?"

"I have to do it," she whispered, gathering strength.

"I am so relieved. I can't believe it. It's all going to work out the way we wanted it to. Father Sean asked to meet me. He had a crisis of conscience at the last minute and told me that I couldn't go through with our plan to switch the babies! Each baby will go to the parents God had chosen for them, he said. So Poppy's baby will go to his nephew Franklyn, after all. I cannot describe how happy I am. I would have had to carry an unbearable secret for the rest of my life."

"...I held her. She is just so charming. So delicate and beautiful in every way. It's obvious that she's going to be a great beauty when she grows up. I smelled her. She smelled just like her mother. The scent of a clear spring day. I handed her over to her

new family. I didn't think it would be so hard, but I have to admit I did weep a little. We've made plans to see her in three months. Poppy. Poor Poppy. She's back home now. Not talking. She never leaves her room. Her moans are horrific to hear. I know what we have done is all for the best in the long run. But right now I feel terrible. Oh, if only I could take her in my arms and explain that in a year from now all of this will be..."

"I can't talk. I can't talk to anyone. Not even Jewell. Not that she wants to talk to me, either. Everything we did in the last months, we did in vain. All of our concern, our secrecy, our planning, has gone down the proverbial drain. Poppy left in the middle of the night. Jewell didn't even hear her. And I know she went to him. After everything we've gone through, despite all the pain and hard work, she went and threw her life away, after all. Just like that. And there's nothing I can do."

With trembling hands, Poppy moved on to the next diary.

"I am so happy. I am so thrilled. We saw Poppy's baby today. They've called her Kate. She's grown so much since we saw her last. She looks just like Poppy did at this age. It's her first birthday, and when her cake was presented to her she reached out and grabbed a piece and shrieked. Her father was holding her, and I was standing nearby in a group of people. But she managed to hold out her little hand to Jewell and offer her a piece and smile. Jewell was tickled pink. So far her heart murmur hasn't presented any problems, and I couldn't be happier."

"...they've moved. We are devastated. Jewell told me she cried all night and Collier had to go into the guest room to sleep. I don't

know what she's going on about. It's not the end of the world. It may be harder to see little Kate now but we can still do it. Franklyn Doyle had to move for his job. Florida is a lovely place to bring up a child, I think. Although, of course, Philadelphia is much better."

"...and it's so hot here. Despite the fact that ladies don't perspire, they glow, I have to admit I am drenched all over. Joy of joys, she is walking now. Really walking, not just toddling around like the last time we were here. She loves the beach. Her father carries her high on his shoulders in and out of the waves and then puts her down to walk alongside him as they collect stones together. She has a beautiful, strong body. Jewell and I agree that she could definitely be an athlete. To think that when she was born I thought she would be sickly! Jewell was in the water next to her today, an arm's length away, when a wave came along and they were pushed together. She talked about it for the rest of the afternoon. Isn't she silly..."

"Jewell and I have bought a small cottage here. It seems a waste to have to put out all that money for a hotel. And of course it makes sense because we will always be coming back here."

"...we talked to her today. We were just strangers under wide straw hats walking together by her front yard. Her mother was there, looking a little piqued, I must say. But she nodded in acknowledgement. Little Kate was having a tea party with several of her dolls—one of them, we noticed with glee, was from us. She was sitting at a little table passing around tiny little cups of tea. Her voice is so sweet, so grown up, and somehow so confident. She is a curious little thing. Jewell says she looks like

170

part our side of the family, part... his. He must be very good-looking, for she is turning into a truly beautiful creature. The soft curls in her hair must be from him, as the rest of us all have hair that is rod straight... Collier hired a detective. Bless that man. He was determined to find Poppy no matter what. Apparently, they are living in New York City on the Upper West Side. In squalor, no doubt. Collier wants to write a letter to her. I am afraid if he does and she doesn't answer, it may break his heart. I don't think Jewell can stop him though..."

"...she's cute without her two front teeth, dressed in her well-pressed school uniform, pigtails in ribbons. Just the way we used to do for Poppy. She was with a little freckled child, who, annoyingly, wouldn't leave her side. Nevertheless, we posed with her for two Polaroid pictures and Jewell gave her one. I don't know what she was thinking. Such a reckless thing to do. We do try and disguise ourselves more and more as she is getting older, with hats and glasses and scarves. We have just come out with our sixth cookbook, which we wrote here. What a mess we make in our little cottage kitchen. We are both at our happiest when we are here. Isn't that strange? It's been 7 years since we last saw Poppy. Jewell said to me the other day, 'The more I miss her, the closer I feel to little Kate. I lost my daughter, and can only find solace in the daughter she lost...' Isn't that strange? I feel the same way."

"A tragedy has happened. Kate's mother has disappeared. In hindsight, we knew something was up. She had been looking rather remote in the last months. We could spit we're so mad. Poor little Kate. Jewell wishes we could just bring her home with us and raise her ourselves. She would be a much better mother than she was to Poppy... and we love her so much. We met with

Father Sean. He told us in no uncertain terms that taking her back would be catastrophic and extremely harmful to her emotionally and psychologically. We are, after all, total strangers to her. He said Franklyn is a good man and is more than capable of bringing up his daughter. Watching them all these years, we must admit that's true. Still, we wish..."

"We've reconnected with Poppy! It was wonderful to see her. She barely said a word to us, though. She has two children, who are..."

When Peter and Poppy came to the end, they closed the last diary and put them all back in the packing box.

"Before you head home," she said, "will you do me a favor, darling boy?"

"Anything, Mom."

"Send these to your sister, Kate. She needs to read them as much as I did."

∞

Like a pair of polished stars destined to explode into a hundred-thousand threads of time, the two of them bathed on the water's edge. Delivered, pardoned, absolved.

Gradually, they began to drift apart. One became the smudged print on a crumpled newspaper carried away on the wind, and the other, a jazzy melody on a radio just plugged in.

But they would always be together, because we are, all of us, one.

The wound is the place
where the light enters you.
- Rumi

CHAPTER THIRTY-TWO

AS POPPY waited for a response from Kate, she did what came naturally to her: she picked up a pen and paper, and began to write. She wrote the first few sentences of her letter to Kate on her way to the airport. The rest of it she finished on the eleven-hour flight from Philadelphia to Prague, where she would meet up with Ari for the final week of shooting. She felt she needed to share as much of herself as she could with Kate. Maybe if she could remember details, specific feelings or moments, and reveal them as honestly as possible, Kate would believe that the meeting in the church couldn't have been a set-up. Maybe she would understand the forces at play in Poppy's life and how they had influenced Kate's. She wanted to connect with Kate in whatever way possible. So she began with her childhood. She wrote and wrote whatever came to mind.

ᵒᵒᵒ

Ari and Poppy were standing on a mountaintop surrounded by a massive medieval castle, an hour outside the city limits of Prague. Three-hundred lights hung from twenty-foot stands in the castle courtyard, and even more were committed to the ancient castle's stone walls beyond. Black-clad crew members made last-minute preparations, and readied themselves to operate the visual effects. The sky overhead was pitch black, with just a twinkling of scattered stars. Only if you turned around and looked up would you see the glowing orb that was the moon, hovering just above the castle spires.

Lucy Semblance had just made an elaborate costume change that had taken longer than anticipated. Now, without warning, she was suddenly ready and standing on the moon in a silvery-golden gown, her long blond hair shimmering in the lights. Everyone turned to Ari. The assistant director grinned at him and looked at his watch. The script supervisor nodded. Jonathan, the cinematographer, gave a wave. He was sitting with the operator on the camera crane, having been pulled up many feet into the sky. And Lucy Semblance was standing in the middle of it all, alone and beautiful.

"Ready?" the assistant director asked Ari.

Ari felt exhilarated. He turned to look at Poppy and gave her a wink. Poppy felt lightheaded with excitement. She reached over and tightly squeezed his hand.

"Action!" Ari called out on a megaphone, and his voice resounded through the mountains and valleys all around them. Then, suddenly, right before Poppy's eyes, the scene she had so very carefully written with tears rolling down her face, the very last chapter in the very last book of the *Luna* series, began magically to come alive. She watched spellbound as twinkling, star-studded steps began to materialize, just the way she had imagined they would several years ago. Each step began to unfold against the dark blue night sky, one, then the next, and then the one after that. Leaving the moon, Luna moved down each step as it appeared miraculously, just in time. Poppy's heart swung and leapt as she watched Luna's golden-clad foot take its very last step, finally resting gently, delicately, and very securely on planet Earth, in front of the magnificent castle.

Just then, Luna looked up to the castle tower, where she noticed a lovely gray-haired lady, seated at a great wheel from which thousands of silver threads were being spun. The very same silver threads that had mysteriously formed themselves into the steps that she had just descended.

The lady smiled at her. And it was this smile that identified her to Luna. She was her mother. Though simply dressed, her smile was so brilliant that it was as though she herself were the sun. Without hesitation, Luna ran into the castle and up the marble stairs. It was halfway up and halfway down, right in the middle, that Luna and her mother met and fell into each other's arms.

"Finally I found a way to bring you home," her mother said. "Finally I have you back again, my dear Luna." She wept tears of joy.

○○○

Late that night, as Ari slept soundly beside her in the enormous bed at their hotel, the last *Luna* shoot finally completed, Poppy was restless. Slipping out of bed, she curled up on the sofa at the end of the room and picked up her letter to Kate.

Ari, your father, was the most attractive man I had ever met. It was the power that he exuded that made him that way. No one ever doubted a word he said. Even though it was more than possible he was making it all up. He was just one of those people who made everyone around him feel confident and capable. There was something else about him, and that was the way he saw the world. His enthusiasm for life was so magnetic I could not keep myself away from him. From the day I met him I wanted to stay by his side. We fell in love and conceived you.

Poppy looked up at Ari. As he slept, the shine from the moon coming in through the curtains set him aglow. It was more than forty years since she had met him at the publishing house in New York City, and she loved and prized him more now than ever before.

Every day after I gave you up, I cried for you. I cried so hard that my body ached. But at night... at night everything was different. At night I had the most magnificent dreams about you. They were so real. To this day I can remember how it felt to touch you and feel your sweet breath on my cheek. When I awoke though, you were gone, and I had to face the emptiness again. It got so I didn't want to be awake anymore.

Putting down her pen and paper, Poppy began to sob, and her entire body shook. Within seconds, Ari was awake, out of bed, and on his feet. He grabbed her and took her in his arms.

"Oh Ari, how could I have let all this happen?" she moaned. She allowed him to hold her and cover her with soft kisses, on her hair, her forehead, and her cheeks. "How could I have been so naïve and blind? It's just excruciating, Ari, that I was not able to protect my own baby. It's too intolerable to even think about. What a fool I was." Poppy's face was twisted with pain. "Oh, Ari," she wept. "What have I done? Kate is right. I don't deserve her love."

Ari continued to hold Poppy in his arms, knowing to be silent in her moment of despair. He did not attempt to advise or dispute her in her hours of grief. Instead, he rocked and kissed her until finally, drained of all emotion, she fell asleep.

Knock and the door will be opened to you.

- Jesus of Nazareth

CHAPTER THIRTY-THREE

DEAR KATE—

Let me introduce myself—I am your birth father—Ari Doumas. We have not yet had the opportunity to meet—maybe we will have that chance someday—maybe we won't—I guess that will be up to you. Your true father—Franklyn Doyle—is the one who is in your heart—and in no way do I want to—or ever could—fill his shoes. But I can reach out a hand to you—a hand that is loving and runs with the same blood as yours—so if by some extraordinary chance you might ever desire the support or comfort of that hand—know that for as long as I walk this earth it will forever be extended to you in hope.

Always yours—Ari

°°°

Kate:

We may never sit across from one another, never share an ice-cold lager and a ripe, red tomato covered in salt that Robert and I grow in the veg garden beyond our shed with our kids. Nor will we, I suspect, ever swim in the pond together near our cottage in the English countryside, only an hour's drive from London, if you are driving with Robert's foot on the peddle. Nevertheless, I thought I might start off this letter by telling you a little about myself, which, I guess, I just kinda did.

I hope you are cognizant of the fact that you have derailed all of our lives because you refuse to even meet us and give us a chance.

No one has the guts to say it in case it will chase you away forever. But I think you need a little nudge. So I will put it to you in the plainest of words. Please let us in. You won't regret it. I promise.

Peter

P.S. May I digress for a sec to thank you for adding a man bag with tons of compartments to your purse collection.

○ ○ ○

Dear sister Kate,

It makes me very happy to know that you are in my life, although I have to admit, I have always felt your presence. But now at least I know we are on the same planet, and that you are no longer high above me, on the moon.

Strangely enough, I have always felt you to be by my side. A phenomenon, I wonder, or just a small girl with a wild imagination who knew you were out there somewhere? Have you, by any chance, had a sense of me? Most probably, you haven't. You didn't know that I even existed until months ago, whereas I have been hearing and reading about you—the fantasy you—all my life. Since the day I could sit still and listen, I remember being told, "This is the story of your sister." And of course, I believed.

I want you to know, I have loved you all my life. And will always continue to do so.

Your sister,

Beatrice

○○○

Beatrice put down her pen. Her letter was written. It was done. Finally.

It had taken her hours to write. Two hours to write two paragraphs and two short sentences. Two hours of struggling to get it right. She had not been insincere when saying she had loved her sister all her life. But which sister had she really been referring to?

Luna?

Or Kate?

The honest answer was Luna, of course.

Kate was a stranger to her. Kate was a trespasser, an interloper. And Kate was a thief who had stolen the sister she knew away.

This new sister alarmed her. This new sister made her anxious. For, this new sister began to stir feelings in her that, for a long time, she had struggled to suppress. Feelings of inadequacy and imperfection had plagued her entire life. Because, compared to Luna, she had always felt second best.

What was she thinking? Beatrice shook her head in irritation. She was a woman in her forties comparing a fictional character to someone real. She had been over this time and again with her parents when she was growing up.

"Of course Luna is extraordinary," her mother would tell her. "She needs to be. She's a fantasy."

"Luna is a figment of your mother's imagination," her father would say. "But you, Beatrice, are not imagined. You are the genuine article."

"That makes you even more extraordinary than Luna," her mother would say sternly. "You can express yourself, and you don't need me to do it for you."

And, in fact, as her parents had encouraged, Beatrice did indeed begin to express herself. So much so, that she had to be reprimanded on many occasions for being *too* outspoken. This outspokenness had led to good things, though. Drawn to politics, she was selected right out of university, to be the head writer on a small Midwest TV news show. From there, her star only rose higher. She married Max, a political cartoonist. They had their sons. They were living in Atlanta now, where she was a head writer for CNN.

Turning to look out the window at her twin boys, who had come over to help their father clean up the backyard, Beatrice wondered about Kate and what she was like.

°°°

They stared at one another, and it was like looking into their reflections in a pond. They lay their hands out on the table between them, and were surprised to find them the same shape and the same size. One pair, however, was manicured, French-tipped and moisturized; the other was calloused and nicked from years of working with leather. They grinned at each other.

They had been born forty-some years ago, two years apart. They shared the same parents, the same brown eyes, the same finely-shaped features, and the same crescent moons over their hearts. But until today, they had never met. They gazed at one another with wonder, not knowing where to begin. They had no shared memories. No shared past. They were just two sisters eager to know one another—and they understood that this knowing would only come with time. They had so much to look forward to.

It was Beatrice's first visit to Florida. She had flown down just to see Kate. Though Kate had said she wasn't ready to meet anyone yet, Beatrice had decided to take the risk anyway. That was her way.

"I'll just stay in a bed and breakfast nearby, and I promise I won't stay long," she had begged. Kate had reluctantly gone to pick Beatrice up at the airport, where they had no trouble recognizing each other out of the hundreds of other faces around them. The moment they set eyes on one another, something exploded in each of their hearts.

"What is the most difficult part of this for you?" Beatrice asked Kate.

"I think..." Kate paused, pursing her lips. "I think that it might be that you have known each other for so long... that you're a *real* family. It will be impossible for me to feel anything other than like I am just tagging along. I feel like the foreigner who'll never really fit in. I'm afraid I'll feel you all are halfway around the race track telling jokes and laughing, and I am so far behind that I can't even hear what's being said."

Beatrice listened, nodding, concern spreading across her brow.

"There is something else, too. My father. I loved him so much. Having Ari as another father, even though he is my birth father, makes me feel like I am betraying my dad." Tears filled her eyes, and she wiped them away.

"And you?" Kate asked. "What is the hardest part of this for you?"

Beatrice hesitated, her hands reaching up to cover her face in embarrassment. "I know this is ridiculous, but I wonder if Mom and Dad will end up loving you more than me."

When Beatrice uncovered her face, Kate could see that tears had filled her eyes, as well. They lay their hands out on the table between them again. This time, their fingers touched. Two so very different hands—yet so much the same.

They both knew that this coming together was just a beginning. It might take a while, it might take weeks, months, years, but they had a starting point and a desire. They knew that triumph demanded both.

***What makes the desert beautiful
is that somewhere it hides a well.***
- Antoine de Saint-Exupéry

CHAPTER THIRTY-FOUR

SLOWLY, Kate became more open to accepting Poppy's letters and calls. After her visit with Beatrice, and after reading the diaries, she had to admit that she no longer believed Poppy had manipulated her, and actually began to crave their interactions. Though, as the entire family would soon learn, triumph demanded far more than a starting point and a strong desire to succeed. It required awareness of conditions that none of them knew to expect. Triumph required intuition and sensitivity. It required calm and composure. And it demanded patience. In the beginning, none of them expected so many obstacles would come their way, believing sincerely that love alone would conquer all.

°°°

Kate and Poppy began to speak daily. They traded photos, favorite quotes, and books. They talked about Poppy's mother and aunt, and Kate wanted to know as much as she could. Her curiosity was unquenchable. As Poppy told her stories about them and their antics, Kate began to see them as the real people they had been, and not the apparitions she knew.

"They were rather fantastic, Kate—if you didn't have to live with them! My father called them his 'rascals.'" Poppy laughed into the computer screen. Kate was in her home workshop, hundreds of miles away, her laptop propped up on a worktable, going through the different pieces of leather that had just arrived from the Hass tannery.

"Oh! I like the sky blue mixed with the bright orange. Have you ever used that combination before?" Poppy called out.

"Never," Kate said, looking into the computer screen and holding up the two different leathers side by side so Poppy could see better.

"Very Mediterranean-looking," she said, smiling. "But I think it needs another color..." She paused, searched out a narrow strip of shiny red from another pile, and held it up with the others. "Just to make it pop. What do you think?"

Poppy clapped her hands together, which made Kate's two Labradors, Lola and Huey, bark. "Well, it's obvious that they like it, too." Poppy laughed.

"What quote do you think I should use?" Kate asked, looking back over her shoulder, where a sizable bulletin board stood. It was covered with hundreds of hand-drawn designs, pictures, leather swatches and notes. Reaching back, she took down several sheets of quotes. "I'll throw out some ideas, and you pick. How about that?" Poppy beamed in response.

"'We need silence to be able to touch souls.' Mother Teresa," Kate began. "And then there's, 'Don't tell me the moon is shining; show me the glint of light on broken glass.' Anton Chekhov. Or maybe..." She hesitated, going down the list. "'It is you alone who must reveal the hidden jewel to the sun.' Charles Munch."

Looking back at the computer screen, she added, "That one, actually, could be a small homage to your mother. Which quote do you think? Or shall I read some more?"

"The last quote," Poppy whispered. "I like that one the best."

° ° °

On another occasion, when a video call was scheduled between Kate and Poppy, it hadn't worked out so well. Accustomed to her other children understanding, Poppy sent Kate a short email delaying the call, thinking that if she got her business calls done first, she could spend more time with her firstborn. Kate, not thinking to check her emails, was so worried when the call from Poppy never arrived—getting no answer when she tried to call her—that she went for a run along the beach to calm down.

Half an hour later, as her cell phone rang, there was a knot in her chest when she answered it.

"Are you okay? I was so worried!"

"I'm sorry," Poppy answered. "I thought I'd just finish up with some business calls..."

"I understand," Kate replied. "Business is important to me, too."

Hearing the hesitation in Kate's voice, Poppy felt ashamed, and promised herself never to do such a thing again. The rules, she determined, had to be different for Kate. The two of them were just beginning to feel their way through this new world of theirs. For the next several weeks, Kate pulled back, and her emails slowed down. She was busy getting out a late order, she explained. Nevertheless, Poppy felt Kate's hurt, and in trying to make up for her mistake, she persisted, sending some little tidbit every day.

° ° °

Kate hid on her birthday. Everyone in her family knew she did this. She hid because she couldn't stand the attention it focused on her. All the pats on the back, the phone calls from faraway friends, the cards that had to be opened, made her shudder and cringe. It was a day Scott and the girls knew to avoid at all costs. But Poppy knew none of this. She sent an elaborate birthday card, champagne, a pin with three crystals shaped like crescent moons, and a huge antique basket filled with wildflowers, like the kinds they had seen on their walks in Paris. When her birthday call to Kate was ignored, and her gifts were left unacknowledged, it gave her pause.

"I have offended her in some way," she told Ari after he found her in tears in their bedroom. Several days later, when Kate did praise Poppy's gifts in a letter and thanked her, Poppy was unsure. She discounted Kate's pronouncements about the basket of flowers being the most beautiful she had ever received, and that the crystal pin with the three crescent moons had made her cry. *Maybe*, she thought to herself, *I overwhelmed her. Maybe in my excitement, I gave her too much. Oh dear God, please don't let me scare her away.*

ooo

Once every two weeks, Kate and Beatrice talked on the phone and they emailed almost every day. It surprised them both that they had so much to say to each other. They talked about politics, about how best to get rid of ants, the best way to housebreak a dog, and sundry other things, important and not.

Kate and Peter met for the first time in London, when she traveled there for a meeting at Harvey Nichols, a luxury department store in Knightsbridge. They had tea together. And he made her laugh. He made her laugh nonstop. She laughed so hard she spilled tea all over herself. Peter was there with a napkin dipped in soda to clean the stain away before she even knew she had done it.

Several months later, they met again. This time it was at his home, Brookside Cottage, in The Cotswolds, where she was introduced to Robert, his partner, and their two children. After a sumptuous, homegrown meal that they all picked from the garden in the back, they gathered around a roaring fire and played Apples to Apples until everyone was bleary-eyed and falling asleep.

ooo

Ari held back as much as he could. Beatrice had told him about Kate's conflicted feelings regarding her father, and he understood. They had talked a few times, rather shyly, and several emails had passed between them. Once, he and Poppy had visited her in Florida for a weekend. But all in all, there remained a distance between them.

And then, one day, out of the blue, after looking at a

final cut of the last *Luna* film, Ari called Kate from the editing room and asked if she would fly up to New York City and help him with something. "Everyone here knows the movie inside and out," he told her. "I need a fresh pair of eyes. Can you help me?" Without hesitating, Kate agreed, and she was on a plane the next day.

The screening room was small, plush and elegant, with thirty luxurious orange velvet seats. They sat side by side, staring at the huge screen, waiting for the film to begin.

"It's just us," Kate said, looking around, confused by all the empty seats.

"That's right," Ari nodded. "It's just you and me."

○○○

Afterwards, the two of them walked down the block to Ari's favorite restaurant, Amaranth. They talked and talked. Ari wanted to know all of her thoughts about the film. And she had a great deal to say. When it was time for her to go, she was surprised to find herself reluctant to part with him. All of a sudden, she felt that it was possible for her to love both her fathers. Love for one, she realized, did not diminish love for the other. She smiled as she remembered a line she'd read in a book many years ago. "Thousands of candles can be lighted from a single candle, and the life of that single candle will not be shortened."

Ari had ordered a limousine to take her to the airport, and the driver waited as he hugged his daughter goodbye. When the car drove away, taking her with it, Ari sat down on the steps of a brownstone nearby, and had a good cry.

"She loved it," he told Poppy later. "And I love her. She's just like you, my sweetheart. Did you know that?

Let us always meet each other with a smile,
for the smile is the beginning of love.
- Mother Teresa

CHAPTER THIRTY-FIVE

HIGH ABOVE the corn and wheat fields, along the ridge of the hill, just where the forest takes over the land at the top and covers everything in seventy shades of green, a hawk flew low, then lower, and swooped something up from the ground. Kate watched as he flew with his catch, up and away, and disappeared out of sight. Ten years had passed since her grandmother's and great-aunt's deaths. She was sitting on the steps of her grandmother's covered porch, morning glories tumbling down about her in great purple multitudes. Kate liked sitting on the porch in the early morning, before the sun was too hot, still in her nightgown, barefooted, a mug of freshly-brewed coffee in her hand, one of her grandmother's books of poetry in her lap. Scott, up before daybreak, was out wandering the hills with his cameras, his tripod slung over his shoulder.

The grand old stone house and the acres of land all around it were hers now. They had become hers and Scott's a year after Jewell and Jane's passing. She was grateful that they had willed the farm to her long before their deaths, and grateful still to have a place for the entire family to gather. She and Scott used the farm as their retreat. They had fixed up the barn and the old house, painting and refurbishing both outside and in, bringing everything back to its original character and charm. During the winter months, when the land was barren and covered with snow, Elwood, Mrs. Kane's great-grandson, who now owned the dairy farm next door, looked in on things daily, checking the furnaces, fixing leaky faucets and roof tiles blown off during storms.

Kate loved the smells on the farm—the scent of freshly-cut grass, corn and wheat, and the whiff of newly-spread fertilizer in her rose and vegetable gardens, that the breezes brought past. She loved planting her vegetables in the spring, and filling baskets with long green beans, lettuce, potatoes and bright red tomatoes, warm to the touch. She loved the first taste of the cream on top of the milk bottle she got next door at the dairy farm. She felt connected here, part of the land. She was a part of something greater than herself and felt rooted in a way she had never been before.

ooo

Off in the distance, she heard the sound of her mother's old station wagon coming up the long dirt drive. *She must have started out early*, Kate thought, putting aside her mug and her book, and standing to greet her. Ari would be coming separately, after collecting Beatrice and Max at the airport.

"Hey, Mom," she called out, the word still new on her tongue after all these years. Unlike most daughters, she never took for granted that she called this woman *Mom*.

"You must have risen at dawn."

"I know, I know. I'm early, but the drive from the Hudson Valley always takes longer than we think. Help me with these grocery bags, will you?" her mother said, as she headed to the back of the car. Poppy had let her hair go silver, which she wore in an elegant twist. She was straight and lean and laughed more easily these days, and the deep wrinkles around her eyes were the lovely evidence of this. After finding Kate, she had been able to branch out in her writing, penning novels for adults now. Kate, too, had branched out. She had a chain of boutique stores in America and Europe.

Tonight, Poppy and Ari would be celebrating their fiftieth anniversary under the stars. Everyone was coming, traveling from far and wide. Their entire family would be celebrating with them.

oo o

"Do you remember when we cooked our first meal together?"

"Yes. Remember those amazing vegetables? That wonderful bottle of red wine?"

"And that heavenly crusty bread?"

"Looking out at our church, with the bells ringing each hour..."

"We were just new friends then... neither one of us knew what was to come."

"Have you ever thought about what life would have been like if you had kept me?"

"So many times."

"But you know what, if you had done anything

differently, we wouldn't have the lives we have now. I wouldn't have had my dad, or Scott, or the girls. And I wouldn't trade them for anything."

"And I wouldn't have written the *Luna* series."

There was a long, wistful silence. They had been in the kitchen together the entire day. Kate, with her long hair tied back, had flour on her face. She was responsible for the homemade bread, the pastries—using recipes from *The Kindliness of Sweets*—and the spread of hors d'oeuvres. Poppy's domain was the main course: crabmeat-stuffed baby peppers and a huge grilled salmon, freshly caught. The risotto and the salad, picked right from Kate's garden, were to be prepared by both. Ari, Peter and Robert, Scott, and Beatrice and Max, were in charge of the wine and the before-dinner mint juleps.

From upstairs they could hear Gwen and Alice, Kate's girls, unpacking, having just flown in from Florida for the weekend. There was shouting and giggling as they caught up with Beatrice's twin boys, who had flown in from Berlin, where they were both working now. Peter and Robert's son and daughter, Daniel and Rose, the youngest of Poppy's and Ari's grandchildren, were up there with them, as well.

At the kitchen window, Poppy and Kate watched Beatrice direct the men, as they maneuvered a long and wide piece of plywood over a pair of sawhorses set in between the two huge silver maples planted almost one hundred years ago, the day Poppy's mother and aunt were born. Beatrice and Peter then carefully spread a huge white linen tablecloth over what was now their dinner table.

Kate put her arm around Poppy's waist. "Why don't we have you and Dad at each end and six of us on one side, and six on the other?"

"I like that. Good idea," her mother replied. "How many bowls of flowers do you think we need? I'll get the twins to go down to the rose garden and cut them. They said they wanted to do something special."

Beatrice came in then, putting her arm across her mother's shoulder, and plucking up a small raspberry tart with her other hand at the same time. "Mmh, that's good, Kate. Just like Grandmother and Great-Aunt Jane would make. And the boys should only cut white roses, don't you think? And don't forget the ice cream I made this morning. It's in the back of the freezer." Kissing her mother on the cheek fleetingly, she grabbed a tray of silverware and napkins from nearby and, standing at the foot of the stairs, called out, "Guys, we need your help down here."

Five minutes later, a line of mismatched, elegant, antique wooden chairs filed out of the house one by one, led by Beatrice. Laughing and happy, their children arranged them around the table. The white roses were placed amid the long row of tapered candles positioned down the center. The final touch was the crystal glasses that had been in the family for generations. And they sparkled splendidly in the late afternoon sun.

∘∘∘

It was twilight. The magic hour. The lightning bugs twinkled here and there, like fairies flying through the night. Everyone wore white. The women were in summer dresses, some short and above the knee, some long, flowing gracefully to the ground, all with bare backs and shoulders, as they had expected the evening to be very warm. The men were jacketless, in dress shirts, some unbuttoned, their sleeves rolled up. The meal had been a great success. Kate's pastries and Beatrice's ice cream had made a perfect end to the feast.

Ari stood up now and tapped his glass with his spoon. All the chatter around him stopped. He popped open a magnum of Dom Perignon, which he poured into the fourteen glasses and passed around to everyone. He had aged gracefully. He was evenly tanned, with graying mid-length, wavy hair. His eyes were the same as ever: large, brown and exuding a great excitement for life. He was still directing films; time had not slowed him down.

Raising his glass, he began. "To my beautiful wife of fifty years. Poppy, my darling heart, the very finest part of me, you are and always will be the true love of my life. And here's to our three gorgeous children. The first of whom was lost to us for too long. Here's to the miracle that finally reunited us all. At this moment, here, now, I feel we are the most blessed family in the world." He hesitated for a moment and looked to the three of them, Kate, Beatrice and Peter, seeing clearly the mark of the crescent moon above each of their hearts. "And here's to the amazing grandchildren you three have given us. You are all so beautiful and wise. What your grandmother and I wish for, more than anything else, is to be around for many more years, to watch you all flourish. To watch you all do what it is you were put in this world to do. If life has taught me anything, it's that we are all connected. How and for what reason we were given to one another, none of us can know. But I will be eternally grateful that we were."

Suddenly, a wild wind blew, bringing with it a downpour of rain. No one ran for cover. They stayed just where they were, shrieking and laughing, as the rain spilled off the silver maple leaves and soaked them all through.

The treasured ones, who had been watching from above, soared together past daydreams, past wishes and past moments yet to be. And time unraveled, bathing in light the trembling, shimmering sea.

CODA

IT'S PROBABLY time for a new car, Poppy thought, as her station wagon lurched out of the driveway. The makeshift table was still up in the yard from the night before. When she got back from the village bakery and the grocery store, she would make sure the guys dismantled it and put it away before everyone went back to their lives. The ice cream that Beatrice had made was so delicious she wished there was some left over. In fact, all the food had been unbelievable, and there wasn't a morsel left.

Dawn was just breaking. It was her favorite time of day. She put on her sunglasses and rolled down her window. The great pleasure of the wind blowing against her face was the best way she could think of to welcome a new day. The roads were empty, and she sped down Route 401 toward the bakery. *Oh, they'll be so surprised*, she thought with glee. When they all woke up, breakfast would be set out for them. She would make sure to get orange juice for Peter and fresh milk for the kids, all of whom still drank milk, only it had to be low-fat now. Ari would need his espresso right after opening his eyes. For Kate, she'd have to remember a latte and a croissant. Beatrice would have only fresh fruits. She was hoping to stop at a fruit stand on the way, maybe get some peaches.

A quarter of a mile from the bakery, while crossing a deserted intersection, what looked to her in that split second like a beam of dazzling light—but elegantly, musically, capriciously transformed into a yellow Mustang convertible—shattered the distance between them in no time at all, crashing into Poppy's old station wagon, folding it up like an accordion.

The pain she felt lasted only a few moments. And then she was gone. Like the fluff on the end of a dandelion, blown away by the breath of a child.

∞

In the beginning, she noticed the lack of resistance. When she breathed, lifted her arms, took her first step. All restraints were gone. She could feel with her mind, think with her heart. She knew that all things were well and right. She spread her arms wide, exposing the edges of her. Her shadow fused and melted into the expanse.

"Where am I?" she asked those gathered around. "You're here. You're back. You're home," they reminded her.

"Ah, yes," she acknowledged.

She began to hum.

∞

It was April 30 in the year 2060. Under the shade of an Acacia tree, not far from the birthing huts in a remote village near Nairobi, Kenya, the capital of the United States of Africa, where years of climate change had unexpectedly left the Maasai Mara lush and verdant, a young woman sat weaving. As custom had it, when the first pain hit, she called out for her mother, her husband, and her sisters. Just as her child was born, a solar eclipse blackened the sky.

The baby was born remembering. By the time she was able to talk, she had forgotten it all.

The wise women of this village predicted that the baby would become a good, fearless leader, and would serve her people well.

ACKNOWLEDGEMENTS

MY father was the author of over one hundred fifty magazine articles and a number of fiction and non-fiction books. While I was growing up, he wrote every morning on his old black Royal typewriter. In the evening, my mother read each word he had written during the day, and with her number 2 pencil, she corrected his spelling, grammar, and edited his text for clarity and purpose. They worked as a team for forty years until my mother's death. They showed me the way.

As a child, I had dyslexia, which made it difficult for me to read and write. My spelling was atrocious and my grammar even worse. I, too, like my father, needed someone who could help me, as I had stories inside that needed to come out. After weeks, months, and years of weaving my web of words and ideas, I needed someone to sit beside me and untangle that web. When I finally found this exquisite person, my entire life changed. Her name is Aida Raphael, and to her I owe so much.

I am also indebted to Andrew Jordan for his brilliant talent for *seeing the entire picture*. He is the architect of the look of this book and the design of its jacket. He puts his heart, mind, and soul into the smallest act. He has magic in his heart.

To Martha Fearnley I am thankful for her insights, her ingenuity, and her ability to hone in on what matters most in a story.

To Diana Sara and Perry Steele Patton for their acumen and generosity.

I am thankful to Irene Fearnley for reading a later draft and graciously offering her time and wisdom.

To Patty McCormack for her meticulous reading of the manuscript and her invaluable feedback, which I took to heart.

Made in the USA
Lexington, KY
23 November 2019